GAME OF SHADOWS

A SEAN WYATT ARCHAEOLOGICAL THRILLER

ERNEST DEMPSEY

JOIN THE ADVENTURE

Visit ernestdempsey.net to get a free copy of the not-sold-in-stores short story, RED GOLD.

You'll also get access to exclusive content not available anywhere else.

PROLOGUE

May 3, 1945
Atlantic Ocean

CAPT. JACK HARRIS nearly jumped out of his bed, jolted from his slumber by a racket he'd not heard in over almost a week. The alarms ringing throughout the ship weren't exactly a pleasant sound when one was in the midst of a deep slumber. Not that he slept deeply anymore. He hadn't in years, not since the war had started. Ever since his ship entered the war, Harris had adapted. He'd almost gotten used to the wildly erratic schedule that changed in an instant when aboard a United States naval vessel. The last week, however, had spoiled him. No enemy sightings and no threats had resulted in several good nights of rest in a row, a phenomenon that now seemed to be at its end.

Exhausted, he swung his feet over the edge of the bunk and quickly strapped on his boots. In mere seconds, he was jogging to the bridge to see why the alarms had been set off. He could have rung the bridge from his quarters, but it was only a thirty-second walk — and a shorter run.

The two hundred men aboard had roused into action. Men manned the big 76 mm guns, turning the barrels in the direction of the nearest danger. The 20 mm cannons were activated as well, ready for the order to open fire.

Twenty-eight seconds later, Captain Harris stepped through the entryway and onto the bridge. "Status," he ordered.

"German U-boat, sir. Off starboard." A young man at a console gave a quick report, but there was an air of uncertainty in his voice.

The bridge was a beehive of activity. Though usually a busy place, now it was humming with men checking instruments, giving reports to officers, making adjustments, flipping switches and turning knobs, and then doing it all again. Off to the side, the sailor manning sonar listened like his life depended on it. His fingers pressed the oversized headphones to his ears to make sure none of the ambient noise convoluted what he was hearing. He picked up a pencil and made a few notations: speed, distance, bearing, even whether or not the U-boat's torpedo tubes had been flooded. The engineers and chief petty officer were on the horn with the engine room in case the captain wanted to change course or adjust their speed. The entire place was in a frenzy.

The room was sterile and lit dimly with red lights to make them less visible to enemy ships during the night. Everything seemed to be made out of gray metal, right down to the seats the sailors were using at the terminals. Naval ships weren't designed for comfort or decor; they were 100 percent utilitarian.

"A U-boat?" Harris asked, grabbing his binoculars and staring out across the rippling waves of the South Atlantic Ocean that shimmered in the bright moonlight. There were only a few wayward clouds drifting through the sky, making visibility extremely good for hunting. "What's it doing this far out?"

"We aren't sure, sir, but at the moment, they aren't taking hostile measures."

There were too many things not adding up in Captain Harris's head at the moment. The first was that they were halfway between South Africa and the northern Brazilian coast. With the war reaching a climactic close in the European theater, a Nazi U-boat being this far out at sea made no sense. The Allies were tightening the noose around the German capital of Berlin. Word was that Adolf Hitler had holed up in his bunker and was doing all he could to muster the troops for one last stand. Some said he had his mistress, Eva Braun, with him in the bunker, along with several of his top advisers.

Germany had no chance of winning the war. It was a story as old as time itself. Hitler should have probably read a little more history. Harris knew plenty. He'd studied a good deal of it at the Naval Academy. One thing he learned early on was that trying to conquer the world was nearly impossible for the main reason that eventually, you'd spread yourself too thin.

Alexander the Great, Xerxes, the Roman caesars, Charlemagne, Napoleon, were all great strategists and leaders, but they all desired too much. Spreading yourself too thin would always create chinks in the armor.

He brought his thoughts back to the U-boat, cruising along off starboard. "How long have you had visual?" Harris asked the young man who'd been feeding him information.

"Just now, sir. When the alarm sounded." The redheaded sailor looked over his shoulder at the captain, worried about what his reaction would be. The kid must have only been twenty years of age, but even he knew that they should have had some knowledge of the sub's whereabouts far sooner than sixty seconds ago.

Harris frowned, his eyebrows lowering. "What do you mean, just now? Nothing on radar or sonar? It just appeared out of nowhere?" The captain tried to curtail his irritation, but in his eyes, either someone was sleeping on the job, they were lying, or they were just plain incompetent.

A dark-haired lieutenant near one of the windows confirmed what the young sailor had said. "He's not lying, sir. All hands were on alert when the ship appeared. Our instruments shorted out momentarily, and then the U-boat was just there."

The story stank, and the man knew it. He could tell from the look on the captain's face that he wasn't buying it. Had the two men corroborated the story? Harris shifted his gaze to the other men on the bridge, but their eyes all confirmed what the other two were saying.

"Ready the charges, man the guns, load the torpedoes," he barked out the orders quickly.

Harris imagined that below deck the men were hurriedly sliding the deadly torpedoes into the tubes and prepping the charge canisters.

He watched with his binoculars, peering through the window at the misplaced U-boat as it continued to glide through the water. He lowered them and stared curiously at the ghostlike ship.

"Why aren't they attacking us?" Harris asked, almost to himself, but within earshot of several of his men.

"We don't know, sir. Like I said, they don't appear to be taking aggressive maneuvers." The kid at the console turned a few knobs and stared at a beeping screen.

The USS *Slater* was a Cannon Class destroyer, mostly built for escort missions of convoys and larger ships. But it still had enough firepower on board, and was maneuverable enough to take down a submarine of almost any size. The Cannon Class was an upgrade from its predecessor, and was specifically designed for antisubmarine warfare. Three hundred feet long and only thirty-six feet at the beam made it fast in the water, capable of reaching speeds of up to twenty-one knots. With three, twenty-one inch torpedo tubes and nine depth charge projectors, the Cannon Class made a meal of enemy subs. And the *Slater* had eaten its fair share.

Harris would have liked to think that the reason the submarine wasn't attacking them was due to its reputation, or simply its menacing appearance. But he knew that wasn't true. While Cannon Class destroyers certainly had claimed many German casualties, the Nazis never seemed to fear anything. It was part of their German heritage. They would press on, charging into overwhelming odds if they had to. At sea was no different. In his time aboard the *Slater*,

Captain Harris had seen a single German U-boat try to take on three escort ships. One of the other destroyer escorts had been badly damaged in the battle, a fight that took over two hours. They'd finally sunk the submarine, though at great cost of time, resources, and a few casualties.

That seemed to be the nature of Nazi sub captains, which made the behavior of this one particularly odd.

"They had to have seen us, right?" he asked the lieutenant standing nearby.

"I would think so, sir," the man in the officer's uniform said semi-confidently. "How would they not? Even if they didn't see us with their periscope, their sonar would be going crazy right now."

Harris knew all of that, and it bothered him. "Shut off those blasted alarms," he ordered. "If they haven't seen us, they certainly would have heard all that racket."

The alarm bells ceased a moment later, and the ship was cast into silence amid the swells crashing against the hull and the low drum of the engine below.

"Where are they going?" Harris said again, this time even quieter than before.

The U-boat was moving quickly to the southwest.

"Come about," the captain ordered. "Tuck in behind them. I want to see what those Nazis are up to."

"Aye, captain. Coming about," one of the officers standing next to the helm confirmed the order.

At three hundred feet, the destroyer was a long ship, but it was able to turn faster than most. Even with that capability, the maneuver to get in behind the U-boat took a few minutes as the ship steered in a wide arch, looping back around into the submarine's fading wake.

"We're in firing range for the guns, sir," the officer standing closest reported.

"We're in range for our torpedoes as well, lieutenant. But I want to know what this sub is up to. If it's a ruse, we'll know soon enough. Hold your fire."

He peered through the bridge's windshield, waiting, watching.

His breaths came in short bursts, a side effect he'd grown accustomed to over the years. It was something that always happened just before battle, a nervous tension that caused a man to tighten up prior to diving headfirst into hell.

The engines continued to hum below as the bow of the destroyer ripped through the Atlantic's swells. The U-boat maintained course as if they had no idea they were being followed. A normal reaction would have been to drop below the surface and try to evade the heavily armed enemy ship. But the German captain made no such effort.

"It's like they're running from something," a young blond operator said from a console on the other side of the room.

"No, son, that boat is modeled from the type IX, though it is much bigger. It's capable of doing at least eighteen knots." He didn't want to say anything to unnerve his men, but it was the biggest U-boat he'd ever seen, at least twice the size of the largest he'd studied or encountered previously. The captain checked their speed on one of the instruments nearby and then returned his gaze to the sea. "We're maintaining with them at fifteen knots. That means they're either on a patrol, or a journey."

The lieutenant's head turned slightly at the implication of the latter. "Where would they be going, sir?"

"I've heard rumors," Harris said. The gruff tone in his voice matched the gray and brown stubble on his face. "You've heard them too, I'm sure. The war is ending, gentlemen. Hitler can't fight forever. There have been reports that indicate some of the higher ups in the German command are trying to escape via submarine." He answered the question of everyone in the room before it was asked. "They'll likely head for South America. And based on this ship's trajectory, that's exactly where they're going."

He waited patiently for another sixty seconds. All two hundred pairs of eyes on the *Slater* watched with tense anticipation. Suddenly, a strange fog began to form, seemingly out of nowhere. The sky above had been perfectly clear, but now faded into a misty gray soup.

"Sir, the instruments," the redheaded sailor said, pointing at his panel.

The captain spun around and glanced at the malfunctioning console. The sonar had lost power. He looked over at the radar operator's station and realized the same thing had happened.

"What's happening to our power?" he asked. A second later, the lights flickered briefly, then died.

"Emergency backup generators, lieutenant," he snapped the order without hesitation.

He could see the man's face in the dark, shaking slowly from side to side. "Everything is down, sir. We have engine power. Nothing else."

Visibility was decreasing by the second. If he waited much longer, they would lose the Nazi vessel in the fog. "Take out their engines with the guns. Fire a torpedo from tube two."

The officer ran out onto the gangway and shouted the orders to the men below. They immediately began relaying the message. The young man at the com grasped the microphone and started to give the order to the torpedo crew, but the line was dead. Whatever was interfering with the ship's power was even knocking out the communication lines.

"It's not working, sir," he informed the captain.

Harris's face grew grave. He'd heard of strange things happening at sea, even seen a few in his time on the open water, but losing every single thing that relied on electricity was an occurrence he'd yet to witness. If the generators went down and the motors weren't providing any current to the batteries, they still had backup battery power that could last many hours.

The guns began to roar at the front of the boat as the gunners opened fire on the fleeing sub. The captain walked around to the side and stood on the grated metal walkway, listening as the gun barrels blazed, flashing bright orange light into the hazy darkness.

In the distance ahead, a white glow seared through the thick fog for a brief second, and then dissipated as quickly as it had appeared.

"Cease fire!" the captain ordered down to the crew below.

They echoed the command through a sequence of other sailors

until it reached the front. The guns went silent again, still smoking from their toils. The sour scent of gunpowder drifted back to the bridge where the captain leaned on the railing.

"What in the blue blazes was that?" he asked quietly.

To his right, the bridge lights blinked for a few seconds and then burned steadily once more. The sounds of the control room resumed with a few clicks, beeps, and pings occasionally escaping from the machinery.

"Sir, everything seems to be working again," the lieutenant reported, stating what the captain had already ascertained.

He stepped back through the entryway and onto the bridge. "Where's the U-boat? Did we destroy it?"

The redheaded man stared at a screen with a line going around in a circle. "It's gone, sir. They must have sunk it."

Captain Harris's face steeled at the news. There'd been no sound of an explosion, no concussion, no resulting waves, and the light he'd seen was certainly not like any he'd seen in his years at sea. Something wasn't right. And there wasn't a doubt in his mind that they hadn't sunk the enemy ship.

"The fog is clearing, sir." The man at the helm pointed out through one of the narrow windows.

Harris spun around and stepped over to the windshield. Just as quickly as it had come, the fog disappeared, making way for the perfectly clear sky, the pale glow of the moon, and calm, rolling tides of the ocean. It was a peaceful scene. Except for an entire U-boat that had disappeared without a trace.

1

Agadir, Morocco

Sean sprinted up the three flights of stairs, taking them two at a time as he ascended. His heart pounded, not just from the exertion, but also from knowing his window would be limited.

He reached the third floor of the hotel, pulled open the stairwell door, and ran straight down the corridor. His room was positioned ten doors down from the end of the hall. Practicality wished it were closer. But he knew it was the only vacancy in the hotel where he could get a clear line of sight.

When Sean arrived at his door, he already had the room key in his fingers and slid the plastic into the slot. The green light blinked twice, and the electronic locking mechanism whined inside the door before it clicked. He turned the latch and rushed into the room.

The interior walls were white, much like the exterior of the hotel. Lavish curtains of purple and gold hung over the windows. The bed featured decorative round pillows sewn from Far Eastern silks of deep red and plush, brown pillows with crisscrossing striped patterns across the surface.

He hurried to the other side of the room and knelt down beside

1

the bed. The blinds covering the balcony doorway were open, letting in the bright early afternoon sunlight. He lifted the comforter and bed skirt, finding the case exactly where he'd left it.

Sean yanked the black golf bag from its hiding spot and flipped off the travel cover to reveal a deadly work of art within. The black Remington M24 sniper rifle was fully assembled and ready to go with a .338 magnum cartridge waiting in the chamber.

He had other rounds, but this shot would only take one.

There were other weapons that could have been used for the job. Popular to many American snipers was the .50-caliber Barrett M82. Truth be told, if he'd been closer to a mile away from his target, Sean might have chosen that gun. Since he was less than three hundred yards, the M24 would do nicely, and was far less cumbersome. Not to mention that he would have had to assemble the Barrett on the spot, and he doubted he would have had that kind of time. Sure, he could have done it beforehand, but if one of the maids decided to ignore the "do not disturb" sign hanging from the latch and happened upon a massive .50-caliber sniper rifle lying on the floor, they would probably have raised a stink, to say the least.

Sean always believed in using the right tool for the right job. On this occasion, the M24 was the right tool.

He checked the chamber to make sure the round he'd left in there was still in position, then relocked the bolt. He deftly moved over to the sliding door and eased it open before getting on his belly and crawling like a snake out onto the stone balcony.

Off to the right, the Atlantic Ocean's waves crashed to the white sand beach that wrapped around the bay. A few tourists, visitors, and locals milled about near the water. Several women were lying out on lounge chairs, soaking up rays from the hot sun. Children's screams of delight and laughter as they played in the ocean foam echoed through the courtyard between Sean's wing of the hotel and his target's. Below, the palm trees lining the paved stone sidewalks and surrounding a green lawn waved in the breeze.

He stopped at the railing, a concrete barricade with dome-shaped miniature arches cut into it in what was a signature design stroke of

Arab culture. If he were on vacation, Sean would have taken a moment to appreciate more of these local subtleties. He'd always found Muslim cities to be most agreeable, and was glad he'd been able to visit them for less stressful ventures than the current one. He reached forward with the sound suppressor he'd taken from the case and carefully screwed it onto the end of the rifle's barrel.

He positioned the tip of the barrel between two of the curvy designs in the railing and propped the weapon on its tripod stand. He flipped open the caps on both ends of the scope and adjusted the sight for his target, a penthouse balcony on the sixth floor of the other wing. Sean checked the wind, which was coming in steadily off the ocean at ten degrees. Not too breezy, but he would definitely have to adjust the shot slightly. He reached up, ticked the scope a few clicks, and then rechecked his angle. The balcony came into view again, more specifically, an empty chair with an ivory-colored cushion. His target would never even know what happened.

It had taken a great deal of patience and resources to track down Gerard Dufort. The Frenchman's disappearing act was hardly a surprise, but how difficult the man had made it to be found was a little unexpected. If Sean Wyatt wanted to find someone, they usually didn't stay hidden for long.

Dufort was slippery, though, using a sequence of back channels and aliases to escape from the mainstream. He'd got away from Sean and his friend Tommy Schultz at Kronborg Castle, also known as Kronborg Slot, in Denmark two months before. Sean was angry with himself for letting the man go. He reminded himself that there was nothing he could have done. The power in the castle went out in a thunderstorm, and in the pitch darkness, Dufort had escaped.

Over the course of the last sixty days, Sean reintroduced himself to the hard training he'd gone through during his first stint with Axis. He'd called Emily Starks, the director of the agency, and told her he would come back to work on a case-by-case basis. Nothing permanent. And totally off the books. Sean had been fighting it for years. He wished he could do something else with his life, but strange circumstances always came knocking on his door, and in the end he found himself doing what he did best: eliminating bad people.

Axis wasn't just a group of assassins, but it was one of the things they could do if the government didn't feel like any of its other arms could take care of it. Axis was small, extremely mobile, and no one outside the unit of twelve agents knew who they were. Each agent was assigned a number, and that number became their name. Since their founding, they'd only carried the numbers one through twelve. Because of his status as an external operative, Sean was given the number zero.

The mission to kill Gerard Dufort was more than off the books. It wasn't even an Axis contract. It was personal; a vendetta against a man who had killed innocent women, sold countless others into a life of rape and slavery, and had never felt the smallest token of remorse for any of it. No, this mission was certainly off the books. And Sean meant to see it through.

Dufort had been clever in his methods. His multiple passports and seemingly endless array of bank accounts registered under fake names and numbers gave him the option to hide nearly anywhere in the world. He'd chosen Agadir, Morocco, a city somewhat off the beaten path by most standards. The choice of country was good enough. It was fairly close to his native land of France, just a short crossing through the Gibraltar Strait. Morocco was a nation of complex culture and vibrant people, making it a much easier place to live than a third world country. And because it was also a tourist spot, but not as popular as the bigger cities of Marrakech, Tangiers, or Casablanca, Agadir made the most sense. It provided all the amenities and luxuries to which Dufort had become accustomed, but less traffic, fewer people, and a location obscure enough to go unnoticed.

Only he *had* been noticed.

The arrogant Frenchman didn't know how to sit quietly and play nice. If he had retired to a life of ease in Agadir, lived peacefully, and never tried anything stupid, he may well have evaded Sean for much longer, perhaps perpetually.

But Dufort couldn't help himself.

After lying low for only forty days, Interpol spotted him coming through a port in Spain. He went through customs with a Spanish passport, probably risking entry into the country so he could get across the border and back into France. For what, Sean wasn't sure. Money stashed somewhere? To reconnect with some of his old cronies? He didn't care why the Frenchman did it. All Sean knew was that it had been the mistake that sealed his fate.

Emily got the call from Interpol, and she relayed the message to him. She'd been willing to let Sean have a go at Dufort since he was still stinging from letting him get away before. It was time to put a salve on that sting.

Sean hopped on a plane from Atlanta as soon as Emily could arrange for one. Working for a beyond top secret team had its perks. Sleek, private jets were one of them. It made things much easier when it came to getting through customs and passing through borders. Ten hours after Dufort was spotted crossing into Spain, Sean was on his tail.

Every day for the last five days, Sean had observed Dufort's every move. He followed Dufort back from Spain, to the Frenchman's condo on the Atlantic. Once Sean knew where the man lived, it was easy enough to procure a room with the perfect angle to observe the target.

One thing Sean noticed was that Dufort enjoyed a cigar and cognac on the balcony of his penthouse every day in the early afternoon at the same exact time. Some Europeans like to have coffee and cake in the afternoon. Others preferred tea. Dufort chose a cigar and cognac.

It didn't matter to Sean what the man was consuming. All he cared about was that the man had a routine, something that could be tracked and counted on at the same time every single day. Little habits like that were things assassins always loved to exploit. Sean hadn't thought that way for a few years, but falling back into his old routine didn't take much effort.

The time he'd spent working security transport for the International Archaeological Agency had kept him on his toes, and several instances over the years saw to it that he never lost his edge; though there were a few moments when it certainly felt like a little rust had settled in. The fact that Dufort was able to get away from him in Denmark certainly shook his nerves, but Sean's high-level training had made his thoughts, actions, and reactions instinctual.

Not now. He was back in the swing, but with a clearer sense of purpose.

Right on time, Sean watched the French double doors swing open to the penthouse balcony, and his target emerged, accompanied by a young girl, probably a prostitute, a muscular man Sean assumed to be a bodyguard, and a butler in a white blazer. While the young woman was a new addition to the routine, Sean was happy to see that his mark had strayed little from his usual course in spite of the new guest.

He set down his binoculars and slid back into position, using the rifle's scope to see the chair Dufort sat in every day so far. With his unassisted eye, Sean watched the group migrate across the balcony to the bar where they helped themselves to a few drinks. The butler poured and then showed Dufort and the girl back over to the right side, closer to the ocean and right where Sean's barrel was aimed.

Sean closed his naked eye and watched his target carefully. He was standing in an awkward position, partially blocked by a concrete piling. The broad railing kept him from getting a clear shot, and at worst, he would only injure Dufort. If Sean fired and missed, or barely clipped the Frenchman, he would surely disappear again, and this time finding him would be a much more difficult affair than the last.

Dufort smiled as he started to move toward the center of the crosshairs in Sean's scope. The target checked his seat to make sure everything was in order and was about to sit down when a knock came at Sean's door.

He froze in place.

Had someone seen him? No one other than Emily even knew he was here. Adriana was off somewhere in Europe, hunting down another priceless work of art. Tommy was busy doing who knew what. Sean wouldn't have told either of them what he was up to, even if they hadn't been in another country. That was just how he operated. The fewer loose ends, the better.

The rapping came from the door again; this time accompanied by a voice. "Room service," the Arabic accent was unmistakable.

Sean's eyes blinked for a second, then peered back through his scope. He'd not ordered room service. Either the bellhop had the wrong room, or Dufort knew Sean was here and had thrown in a wildcard. He hoped it was the prior. Deep down inside, he already knew it was the latter. Knowing the danger lurking out in the hallway, he risked a quick glance over at the bed where his pistol rested in a black case.

He returned his stare to Dufort, who for some reason seemed to be hesitating about sitting down. Sean noticed him motion for the girl to take the seat where he usually sat. She accepted, taking the position squarely in the dead center of Sean's crosshairs.

"Oh, come on," he whispered to himself.

The knocking came a third time, harder than the previous two. "Room service," the voice announced again.

"I didn't order any room service," Sean said loudly, trying to project his voice through the empty room. "Check another room."

There was a silent pause before the bellhop spoke again. "Room service for Mr. Wyatt?"

Sean swallowed hard and kept his eyes on the target. Dufort was moving around, keeping behind the concrete pillars, which made getting a clean shot nearly impossible. Why was he changing his routine all of a sudden? That combined with the knocking at the door could mean only one thing.

Sean didn't want to admit the possibility, but there was no denying it.

He'd been made.

2

Agadir, Morocco

Sean spun around onto his backside just as the door to his room burst open. Whipping the long rifle around took a second longer than he would have liked, but it was still fast enough to squeeze off a round before the intruder in the blue T-shirt could train his weapon.

Sean squeezed off a shot from the hip, with the butt of the rifle wedged between his bicep and his ribcage. The extended barrel puffed loudly. The powerful round struck its mark in the man's chest and went out through his back. Red spots instantly splattered on the hallway wall behind him as he took two staggering steps back and fell prostrate on the floor.

Another man peeked around the corner with a handgun, a silencer on the end of it. He popped off five extremely quick shots, two narrowly missing Sean's feet. Sean wiggled back a few inches and propped himself against the railing. The gunman's hand was holding his weapon just at the edge of the doorframe, which meant his body was probably only eight to ten inches to the left behind two layers of drywall and some insulation.

Sean raised the rifle to eye level and pulled the trigger. The bullet zipped through the thin walls and was immediately followed by a grunt and a thud on the other side. He waited for a few seconds, keeping the barrel of the rifle pointed at the open doorway in case there were more of them. When no one appeared, Sean took a quick look back across the massive courtyard to Dufort's penthouse.

It was empty.

"Crap," he said to himself. He shifted onto his feet but remained in a crouch. It was entirely possible that Dufort had a sniper of his own on the other rooftop or on a balcony in the other wing.

He crept hurriedly over to the bed and dropped the big gun onto the cushion inside the still open carrying case. Next to it was another, smaller case. He flipped open the latches and withdrew his black Springfield XD .40-caliber and slid a fully loaded magazine of hollow points into the handle.

When it clicked, he pulled back the slide to chamber a round.

Sean rushed over to the door, past the hit man's body, and peeked around the corner and down the hallway in both directions. The corridor was empty, save for the other dead man on the floor.

Definitely not a good day to be one of the maids on duty.

He took off down the hall toward the stairwell. An elevator would be too slow. As he reached the door, the latch turned and started to open. He jumped back and aimed his weapon as the gap between the door and its sill widened.

A terrified old man in a red jogging suit with a bottle of water appeared in the doorway. His eyes were wide with surprise and fear. Sean let out a sigh and lowered his weapon, motioning the man through.

"Sorry," he said shortly. "Hotel security. Someone stole some towels."

The old man raised his eyebrows and scurried away, going through the first door on the left. *At least he probably didn't pay any attention to the body farther down the hall*, Sean thought. Sean shook his head and stepped into the stairwell, but was halted by a man in a white T-shirt and khakis. He looked to be of Arab descent, with dark eyes and bronze skin overlapping bulging muscles.

The sinister expression on the man's face told Sean everything he needed to know. Reinforcements had arrived.

He tried to raise the Springfield, but the man countered, chopping down on Sean's wrist then grabbing it with a vice-like grip. He pulled Sean close and swung his elbow at his face.

The pain screeched through Sean's jaw as the elbow struck squarely. The man still didn't let go of his wrist, and punched hard with his fist. The attack hit Sean in the abdomen, instinctively causing him to double over. A knee shot up quickly, aimed at Sean's chin, but he was able to regain his wits fast enough to tilt his head to the side. He reached out with his free hand, grabbed the man's knee pit, and leveraged his weight along with the attacker's to throw him off balance.

The man's reaction was immediate. Even as he stumbled backward and into the railing, he chopped down with his free elbow. It ended in a deep thud against Sean's shoulder blade. Even with the sharp pain suddenly searing through his back, Sean kept pumping his legs, driving the man backward on one foot. The hit man realized what was happening and let go of Sean's wrist in a panicked attempt to brace himself against the railing.

His hand touched the white metal tubing, but the palm slipped over it as Sean pushed the guy back and forklifted him up. There was a brief yelp as the man's big body toppled over the edge and down the narrow shaft between the stairs. He fell headfirst to the hard concrete below, the short fall ending in a sickening smack.

Sean gasped for a second, each breath sending new pain through his back and stomach. He twisted his jaw for a moment, trying to loosen the muscles that had been struck so hard. He leaned on the rail and stared down at the body lying below, the neck twisted at a grotesque angle.

Sean composed himself and took off down the stairs, bounding over them three at a time, nearly twisting his ankle on one as he clipped an edge upon reaching the second floor landing.

He pushed on and jumped the last four steps to the bottom floor, almost falling to the concrete with his hurried landing. He corrected his balance and darted past the body, reaching the door to the back of the hotel wing. As he sprinted through the back parking lot along the rear wall, he was careful to keep his weapon hidden from public view. The last thing he needed was a bunch of screaming tourists panicking and running for cover.

A woman in a white dress exited her BMW 5 Series, holding an expensive-looking handbag. She saw Sean jogging by but paid him little mind. When he rounded the corner, he sped up again for a few seconds before having to slow down once more due to a cluster of pedestrians strolling leisurely down the strip.

He pressed the gun close to his body, tucking it under his shirt as he walked as fast as he could toward the hotel's other wing. If Dufort were going to try to get away, he would have to use this road. Odds are he would go north.

If Sean could get to the other hotel entrance in time, he could cut Dufort off at the resort's only entrance/exit.

It was a good plan. And it probably would have worked had the dead guy in the stairwell not slowed him down. Unfortunately, he was too late. He watched as a black Mercedes sedan whipped out of the garage's other entrance and onto the road. The windows were tinted, but he knew from the way the car was speeding off who was inside.

Sean had purposely left his car close to the road in case he might need to get away. Now, his foresight paid off. He turned around, dashed back toward the rear of the hotel's north wing, and rounded the corner. He reached into his pocket, thankful he'd not set his keys on the desk in the hotel room when he returned earlier.

Thirty feet from the white Jaguar F-Type, he tapped the unlock button on the keyless entry. The car exploded in a ball of searing orange flame and black smoke. The concussion knocked Sean off his feet and sent him plowing into the asphalt, shoulder first.

He winced at the pain pulsing from his shoulder. It mingled with the ache from the injuries he'd incurred during the fight. The heat from the burning wreckage melted over his skin, making the heat of the late spring sun seem like a cool autumn day.

Sean pushed himself up from the ground and dusted off some dirt and debris from his shirt and pants. His messy blond hair had a few pieces of broken glass in it, and he had to run his fingers over his scalp a few times to get them all to shake free. A siren blared in the distance, signaling that someone had just alerted the authorities to the parking lot blaze.

The last thing he needed was to get nabbed in Morocco. While he was technically doing something for Axis, it wasn't exactly on the books. Getting him out might present a certain level of difficulty, even for Emily.

He remembered his weapons and the dead bodies on the third floor. Someone must have seen the carnage by now. He checked his watch. It was only 2:00 local time, one of those periods in a day when very few people check in or out of a hotel. If a staff member hadn't seen the bodies yet, there was still the possibility that he could get out.

Sean raced back into the building through the rear entrance. He grabbed the body at the base of the stairs and dragged the man over to a dark corner underneath the lowest staircase. Several empty boxes were stacked against the wall beside a Coke machine and he quickly grabbed them and piled them around the dead man, effectively hiding him from a casual observer. Someone would find him eventually, but that wasn't Sean's problem. The present was what he worried about.

There was still some blood on the concrete, which he covered by disassembling one of the boxes and flattening it over the mess.

He ran up the steps, pushing himself to ignore the pulses of pain coming from his shoulder, abs, and back. When he reached the third floor, he warily pushed open the door and peered through the slit. The coast was clear, at least for the moment. The body still lay in the hallway against the wall near his room.

Sean eased the door open a little more, making sure no one was hiding in the opposing corners, then he made a break for it. He ran fast down the corridor, reaching his doorway in a matter of seconds. He hurried around the foot of the bed, picked up the rifle, and dropped it on the mattress. A tan canvas rucksack sat next to the two cases, and he bent down and picked it up as well then set it next to the big gun.

His hands worked like a blur, dismantling the weapon into several pieces before stowing them all in the rucksack, along with his handgun.

The sirens drew ever closer. From the sound of it, they were probably less than a half mile away.

Sean rushed back into the hallway, gripped the body by the ankles, and dragged him into the room, laying the arms over the top of the man's partner. He slung the rucksack over one shoulder and his backpack over both, then reached into his pocket for a lighter he kept handy for just such occasions. He hopped back onto the bed and ignited the lighter, holding it close to the sensor on the sprinkler system unit overhead.

Almost instantly, water spewed from the little round piece in an umbrella shape, and new alarms started bleating in the hallway. Sean jumped down from the bed and peeked into the hallway. The sprinkler system on the entire floor had activated, soaking everything. The bloodstains on the wall across from Sean's door began to run, a convenient byproduct of his ploy to get out unnoticed.

Hotel patrons started appearing in the corridor, wondering what was going on. Some appeared to be getting ready for the beach; others looked as if they'd just been asleep. In total, there were only nine other people on the floor at the moment. Not exactly a ton of cover for Sean's escape, but it would do.

He carried his sunglasses in his hand, not wanting to draw more attention to himself by being the guy who wears sunglasses indoors. He took the stairwell, following the other visitors down the same stairs he'd just been on twice before. In the stairwell, people from the floors above and below mixed on the concrete steps. They made an orderly, if not confused, procession downwards. Most of the patrons probably thought it was a drill, though they would have to have been nearly dead not to have noticed the explosion in the parking lot that surely rocked the building. Once they reached the bottom, Sean waited to see if anyone would notice the cardboard on the floor or the boxes stacked under the stairs. Sean was concerned someone might inadvertently kick the flattened cardboard, thus revealing the bloodstain underneath, but it never happened. No one seemed to pay any attention to it. They were too intent on obeying the rules and evacuating the building. Some hurried more than others on the off chance it wasn't just a drill.

He mixed in with some of the other people and made his way back out into the hot sunlight, sure to slip his sunglasses on to help keep from being too identifiable or memorable.

As hotel concierges ushered people through the exits and to the front of the building, Sean picked up his pace, slipping through the mass of bodies and trying not to bump anyone with the rucksack that held his weapons. People gawked at the flaming car that was now being tended to by firemen from the local department. Two police cars zoomed by with sirens screaming, which caused more than one person to cover their ears.

The people were herded toward the north, down the sidewalk away from the building. It was an international standard protocol in case of a fire evacuation, and one that Sean was happy to take advantage of.

A man in a white jacket with a hotel name tag attached to the left breast held up a sign that told everyone where to rally for the evacuation. Sean allowed some of the patrons to start collecting in a huddle around the man and then kept walking down the strip.

He never glanced back. He didn't need to. No one would recognize him or even remember that they'd seen an American in sunglasses with a backpack and a second bag. Why would they? They were too enthralled by the roiling black smoke pouring from the car.

Somehow, Dufort had got wind of his presence, something that now nagged at Sean's mind. The Frenchman had got away from him twice. Maybe the time away from the agency had made Sean rusty. To him, that only meant he would have to train harder.

As he strolled down the street, keeping his eyes peeled for the next taxi, he heard the phone ringing in his pocket. Odd timing for a phone call.

He pulled it out and glanced at the name. It was Emily. He hit the talk button and put the device to his ear, hoping she wasn't calling about Dufort. She had connections everywhere, but no way had she already heard about his mark getting away.

"Hello, Em," he said, turning his head toward the ocean, squinting into the bright sunlight. A group of Asian tourists was on the other side of the road pointing at the hotel where smoke continued to pour into the clear blue sky.

"I'm sorry to bother you on your vacation, Zero, but I need you to come in."

He laughed at her insinuation. "I wish I was on vacation."

Another fire engine whined in the distance. "What's that noise?" she asked. "Do I even want to know?"

"Dufort got away. Pretty sure he tried to blow me up. All he managed to do was make a wreck of my very nice rental."

"He got away?"

"I'm fine, though. Thanks for asking."

"I figured you would have dispatched him two days ago."

"These things take time, Em," he said coolly and stole a quick glance back at the chaos as he turned down a side street, effectively disappearing from view.

"Well, you'll have to pursue him later."

"I plan on it. What's so pressing that you would have pulled me off him?"

"Order from the president. Get to Frankfurt. Let me know when you arrive. I'll pick you up and brief you there."

The phone went dead, and he looked down at the screen. She'd ended the call without much fanfare. Her directness was one of the things Sean liked best about Emily.

He took a deep breath and exhaled slowly. It seemed like every part of his body was hurting. Now he was heading to Germany and had no idea why.

An old, beat up Toyota rounded the corner. The words in Arabic on the side indicated it was a cab. Sean held up his hand and waved to the driver.

Back in the game, he thought, pushing away a twinge of regret. He got in the car and told the driver where to go. The man nodded and sped away, leaving the chaos behind to the voyeurs.

3

Washington, D.C.

Adm. Corbett McClain stared across the Resolute desk with tired eyes. The president had called him in earlier that morning while the admiral was still brewing his coffee.

"Less than twenty hours ago, a terrorist group known as the Black Ring broke into a research facility in Lucerne, Switzerland, and abducted a scientist by the name of Franziska Ott. She's local to the city of Lucerne. According to that report," he pointed at the paper in the president's hands, "she was working on a high-security project that deals with quantum gravity and magnetism."

His sagging eyes, set amid age lines, a high wrinkled forehead, and a broad jaw, told the tale of a man who'd been around the block a few times. The various medals on his uniform gave many of the details to that story. While he didn't know much about the science featured in the report he'd given the commander in chief, he knew enough to realize when something was grave.

President John Dawkins scanned the sheet of paper in his hand. His light-brown hair had streaks of gray in it. The skin on his face had grown looser over the years, but he still had the rugged good looks that endeared him to so many people. It was nearing the end of his first term, though few people believed he would lose a bid for a second. The other party was scrambling to find a sacrificial lamb to throw out into the ring, but it seemed no one was willing to be humiliated by what was sure to be a landslide election. There were, of course, nominations of candidates, but they would see less than forty percent of the votes.

He'd helped bring about a peace between the legislative and executive branches of the United States government, and together they had accomplished more than he'd anticipated. His casual yet stern, no BS way of leading was something others couldn't deny.

For the most part, Dawkins preferred not to get involved with military matters. Men like the admiral were the ones with more experience in those sorts of things. He scrutinized each member of the Joint Chiefs, as well as the rest of his advisers, with a heavy magnifying glass. Having trustworthy people around was one of the things Dawkins valued most.

Admiral McClain had brought in a report that was troubling. A physicist had gone missing in Switzerland. Initially, that might not have been something the United States should have been concerned about. However, the scientist's projects were believed to be high security. Either that meant she was working on something that could be weaponized by enemies, or it represented a significant danger to America or its allies.

The president finished reading the report and laid it on the desk. "You're certain about this?"

"Yes, Mr. President. Our scientists believe that she could have been very close to a breakthrough in that field, as crazy as that may sound." The admiral answered with no emotion, only looking to relay the facts as he saw them.

Dawkins leaned back in his chair. "It's like something out of a science fiction movie, if that information is correct."

"I'm aware of that, sir. But we don't want to mess with these terrorists. The Black Ring is known for upping the ante when it comes to brutality. I fear for what they've already done to Dr. Ott, much less what they will do."

The Black Ring was a European-based terrorist cell. They were hard to track and even more difficult to study because they didn't act like other terrorist groups. While most Islamic militants used various forms of aggression to further their religious war, the Black Ring performed acts for a variety of reasons, some of which were curiously capitalist, despite their clearly communicated disdain for Western economic philosophy.

"What would a bunch of terrorists want with technology like that?" the president asked, staring through the admiral's calculating eyes.

"We're not completely sure. If what that report says is true, some of the theories include cloaking of entire vessels, planes, tanks, pretty much any kind of vehicle. On the furthest end of the spectrum, well, you read the details. The implications are potentially very dangerous."

"I'd say all of it is dangerous, Admiral."

McClain didn't disagree, but merely nodded. "How would you like us to proceed, Mr. President? I can have a SEAL team on it within the next six hours."

Dawkins shook his head. "No offence, Admiral, but we don't even know where to send a SEAL team right now. These animals could be hiding anywhere, and we don't have the foggiest idea of where to start."

"Then what will we do? Sit around and wait until they send us footage of cutting the poor girl's head off?"

"No," Dawkins said, his tone grave. "No, we won't be doing that. As soon as I got wind of this and saw the video of Dr. Ott in a basement with her hands tied behind her back, I made a phone call."

A brief second of concern crossed Admiral McClain's face. "You made a call? CIA?"

"I decided to leave Langley out of this one, Admiral."

"But certainly they know about the video and the kidnapping."

The president shrugged and crossed one leg over the other knee.

"Of course they do. Heck, the entire world knows about it thanks to the Internet. I'll let Langley do what they do. But I've got another asset in play that could well reap faster results than the big machine that is the CIA."

McClain looked pensive for a moment as he considered what the president was saying. Another asset? What other assets did he have? FBI didn't get involved with things of this nature unless it was in the country. NSA? Surely not. He'd heard rumors about other, higher security special operations units working for the government, but most of what he'd heard was the stuff of urban legend.

One name did continue to pop up. "Called in an Axis agent, eh?"

The president's face remained stoic, as if he'd just bet all his chips in a high stakes poker game.

"This isn't a covert hit, Mr. President. We need someone to be able to track down these people and get that young woman out alive. The SEALs are just as good at that as anyone."

"Almost anyone," Dawkins corrected. "If our asset needs backup, he'll let us know, and then you can send in your SEAL team."

It was nearly an insult, but the president meant nothing by it. The admiral doubted the faith his leader put in one agent, led by what he considered to be a shadowy special ops organization. His place wasn't to question the president, though, and he nodded his approval.

"If that is what you believe is the best course of action to take, sir, I am fully behind you."

"Good," Dawkins said and stood up. He extended a hand as McClain also stood, and the men shook briefly. "As always, Admiral, I'll keep you in the loop with any progress that's made."

"Thank you, sir," he said appreciatively.

The admiral showed himself to the door and exited the Oval Office, into a room awash with clerical workers pecking away at keyboards, and other people hurrying about in a dozen different directions.

A Secret Service agent standing outside the door gave a curt nod to the admiral, who returned the gesture before stalking out of the office and through the main corridor toward the front of the building.

He took a left at the main foyer and followed the hallway out to one of the side exits and proceeded outside to one of the security stations.

The Secret Service detail allowed him through in quick fashion, one of the perks of being an adviser to the president. He circled around to the private parking area, got into a black Lincoln Town Car, and turned on the ignition.

He felt his phone vibrate in his pants pocket and retrieved it to see who had messaged him. The number was unidentified, but he knew who it was. There was only a question mark on the screen.

He tapped away at the keys for a few seconds and then sent his two-word response.

Sit tight.

4

Frankfurt, Germany

Sean strolled out of the Frankfurt International Airport, weary from his journey. Even taking a private charter with all its amenities was still traveling, and traveling always seemed to wear him out.

He noticed a blacked out BMW with heavily tinted windows, not unlike the one Dufort had escaped Agadir in less than twenty-four hours ago.

This time, the front passenger window rolled down, and he could see Emily in the driver's seat. She motioned for him to get in. Sean opened the back door and plopped his bags inside before joining her in the front. The door had barely closed behind him when she stepped on the gas and accelerated down the airport street.

"Nice to see you too, Emily," he said, hurrying to put on his seatbelt.

She raised an eyebrow and passed him the slightest grin. "Always a pleasure, Zero."

"Do you really have to call me that? I just picked it because of the whole twelve agents thing and I sort of work outside their..." he fumbled for the word, "boundaries."

"Actually, I was going to assign that to you anyway. You know the protocols, Sean. When you're on assignment, I will only refer to you as Zero." She paused for a second. "Except for just then when I called you by your name. And you know what you have to call me." The last part carried a little playful edge to it.

Sean sighed. "Yes, Director."

The BMW zoomed around the curved on-ramp to the Autobahn and merged into traffic behind a shipping van. A few seconds later, after a gray Volkswagen passed them on the left, she changed lanes and sped up.

"So," Sean said, watching as Emily left the slower vehicles behind on the right, "you were a little skimpy on the details as to why I'm here right now."

"You know me. I prefer to talk about that sort of stuff in person."

"Worried about bugs, are we?" He grinned, but his question carried serious implications.

"Never know," she said. "Better safe than sorry."

She guided the car back into the right lane once they'd passed all the slower drivers, allowing a red Ducati 899 Panigale to zip by. Sean stared longingly at the motorcycle, as if he'd just seen the most beautiful woman on the planet walk by.

Emily went on. "Yesterday, a Swiss research scientist by the name of Franziska Ott was abducted from her lab in Lucerne. A few hours later, a video was released online. It featured the young woman, bound and gagged."

"Confirmed it's really her?"

"Yes. Facial recognition software analyzed the footage. She was taken by a terrorist organization known as the Black Ring."

Sean gave a nod, now staring forward down the road. The overcast skies above looked as if they were about to burst with rain. "I've heard of them," he said. "Shady, even for a terrorist group. They've been rebuked by other jihadists for being capitalistic. I guess the others don't feel like eating is important."

She addressed his humorous comment with a dry observation of her own, apparently not in the mood for laughs. "It isn't when dying is the secondary goal. Still, seems like a racket if you ask me. Now it seems they want something from the professor." She pulled out her phone and handed it to him. "Press play."

Sean did as told and watched the short video clip of the woman in her lab coat, gagged with a rag in her mouth and her hands behind her back. She was on her knees in what appeared to be a damp basement. A single lightbulb hung from the ceiling in front of the woman, and a wet line proceeded down the concrete blocks behind.

Sean finished watching the video, listening to the demands of the kidnappers. He handed the phone back to Emily. "Well, at least we know they're not in the Middle East."

Emily frowned, her eyebrows knit together. "What do you mean? How do you know that?"

"In fact," he said, ignoring her question, "I'd go ahead and rule out some of the African nations as well. Definitely Somalia. I'd say Libya and Egypt are probably out as well."

"How do you know that just from watching ninety seconds of footage?" she asked, incredulous.

"First of all, isn't that one reason you love me? I'm observant. Secondly, that kind of masonry work doesn't occur in the areas with a high Arabic architectural and engineering influence. It's European, probably an Eastern Bloc country, somewhere wet."

"Why is that?"

"The line of water streaming down the cinder blocks behind the woman. It's either a very damp place, or there's been a lot of rain there lately. In both cases, that probably eliminates a lot of the dryer climates."

Her lips parted into a thin smile. "Impressive."

"Thank you. And I know."

"That narrows it down to only a few million possibilities. And according to the man in the ski mask on the video, they're going to kill her in three days."

Sean pushed on, in spite of her cynical response. "Check the weather across all of Europe to start. Look for anywhere that has been rainy for the last day or two. That should help narrow the search field a little. It's not much but it's a start. Last I checked it hasn't been a particularly wet beginning to summer."

Emily nodded. "Makes sense. Anything's better than nothing at this point."

"Also, what was it that she was working on? It seems odd that a group of terrorists would put out a video, claiming what they would do to the hostage without asking for something in exchange. Doesn't that strike you as strange?"

"It does," Emily agreed. "And they did ask for something. From what we know, Dr. Ott was working on something in the field of quantum gravity, something to do with big magnets and a bunch of physics stuff that I don't understand. What I was able to glean from the briefing is that her research could lead to extraordinary advancements in the fields of deep space exploration, cloaking, and any number of other things. It seems they're interested in something she has or had in her possession. We're not sure. They sent an encrypted message with the video, low level, nothing anyone else would see. They're demanding we recover whatever it is she's hiding. Problem is, we don't know what she's hiding or where it might be."

It was Sean's turn to be confused. "Sounds like heavy stuff. You said one of the implications could be cloaking. As in, invisibility?"

"Maybe. I would guess it has more to do with radar and sonar than anything else. A kind of stealth technology, if you will."

Sean snorted. "Stealth has been around for a while."

"Not like this. Her work would effectively make any object, small or large, impossible to detect with standard instrumentation. If terrorists were able to get their hands on something like that, it could mean big trouble."

Sean considered the possibilities. A device of that kind would mean anyone could fly a plane right into any airspace they wanted. They could steer a ship right into the Hudson, park it next to Wall Street, and blow the whole thing up. He still had questions, though.

"One, is that even possible? I'm no expert in physics, but I've dabbled in it. How would something like that work? And two, not to repeat this, but why in the world are the terrorists broadcasting that? If I were them, I'd keep a lid on this one as much as I could."

"Maybe they're trying to make a statement. When was the last time a terrorist did something that actually made any sense?"

"Good point."

"But yes, they are acting differently than most known cells. As to the facts behind those weird, science fiction things I mentioned, our experts are suggesting that she was on the edge of a breakthrough that would change what we know about physics forever. It might have even brought about a unified field theory between classical physics and quantum mechanics."

Sean's eyebrows rose involuntarily. "That's impressive."

"Considering no one has been able to do that so far, not even some of the brightest minds in the world, yes, I would say that's an impressive accomplishment."

The car went silent for a minute. Off to the right, the downtown area of Frankfurt passed by, a powerful reminder that German commerce and economic power still had a strong foothold in the region.

"It's well within the character of Black Ring to do something like this," Emily said finally. "To flaunt the fact that they have a scientist that could change the world for the better and potentially take humanity to the very far reaches of space is a huge power play for them. They're taunting the Western world."

"They want to sell that technology for their own, greedy devices." Sean said. "That's the only thing that makes sense. They're going to have that scientist create something like what you described. With that, they can sell it to anyone in the world. They'll make billions, maybe more if they sell to China."

"Or worse," Emily added.

Sean grimaced at the comment. "True. There is the other communist country." He paused for a second and then asked, "What's my play?"

"I'm taking you to Lucerne and dropping you there. You'll need to go through Dr. Ott's research, her personal things, her apartment, anything that might give you a clue as to what specific project drew the interest of Black Ring."

"Okay," he said after a minute of contemplation. "I assume I'll be able to use whatever resources I deem necessary."

"This mission is highly classified. So long as you don't blab your mouth about who you're working for, I don't care how you get the job done."

"Good enough," he said. "Oh, and by the way, that video has had over ten million views on YouTube, so the mission isn't really that classified."

She shook her head at him with a smug grin. "They don't know about you. No one does but me." The car went silent, save for the hum of the tires on the pavement beneath. For several minutes, neither of them said a word.

In the distance, a castle loomed on top of a hill, a shattered and ruined remnant of its former might. Villages sprang up seemingly everywhere. Some of them had been homes to people of this area for nearly a thousand years. Thick forests of lush, green trees stretched out between the farms. A few massive windmills dotted the landscape, providing power to the growers, their white blades swinging around in slow, wide circles.

Sean spoke up, breaking the long silence. "It could prove difficult to find this...Dr. Ott, Emily. I might be a bit rusty."

"You'll be fine," she said quickly, brushing aside any doubts he may have had. "And you will find her. You're the best. That's why I chose you for this mission. No one else I know of has the mind of a detective and is capable of...." She stopped herself midsentence.

"Killing the way I do?" he finished the sentence for her. "Em, I admit I'm good at it, but there are others out there who are better than me."

"Surviving the way you do," she corrected. "Like I said, no one has the combination you have. And besides, you're one of the only people on this planet I can trust."

The words hung heavy in the cabin for a minute before he responded. "You can always trust me, Em. And you know I'll do whatever I can to get that woman back."

"I know you will." She took a deep breath, shrugging off any emotions she might have been feeling. "You have less than seventy-two hours. The terrorist said they would kill Dr. Ott in three days. That was over twelve hours ago. So you're on the clock. No pressure. Oh," she caught herself before she finished what she was saying. "If I had to guess, I'd say wherever you go, they'll likely follow."

"Always nice to have fans."

"The terrorists are looking for something they don't know how to find. They believe that Dr. Ott can tell them where it is. Up until this point, she has evidently refused. If she continues to hold out, at least they'll have plan B in play. That's you." She jerked a thumb in his direction. "If it has anything to do with something historical, they might know that you would be a perfect answer for the problem. Your reputation, after all, does precede you. That means you'll need to watch your back. It's highly plausible that the leaders of Black Ring know about your exploits and want to use you for their efforts. Once you find what they're looking for, they'll execute you."

"Perfect."

Find a scientist's secret...whatever it is, with no leads as to its whereabouts. Save her from a barbaric group of terrorists. Kill said terrorists. Get the woman back to safety. And all in around sixty hours. Oh, and survival is a bonus.

Good to be back in the game, he thought cynically.

Something still bothered him. "They made that video public."

"Correct."

"But if I'm their plan B, that means they've reached out to our government with their demands aside from that encrypted message."

"Bingo."

"Which means if I find what they're looking for, we have a way to contact them?"

"Right again."

Sean shook his head. "I was kind of hoping I could ease back into things with you," he said in a weary voice.

Emily laughed. "You know it doesn't work that way."

She was right. He did know.

Might as well dive right into the fire, he thought.

5

Lucerne, Switzerland

Sean shuddered and woke abruptly as Emily guided the car out of a mountain tunnel and into the outskirts of Lucerne. He'd leaned his chair back a few hours before, with the permission of his boss, and taken a nap. The journey from Frankfurt to Lucerne was drivable in just under four hours. It seemed like a long time to be in a car, even considering the speeds the Autobahn allowed.

He rubbed his eyes and looked around. During the course of the journey from Frankfurt into Switzerland, the weather had cleared up. The sun shone brightly in a nearly cloudless blue sky. The city of Lucerne had been built at the base of the Swiss Alps and next to Lake Lucerne. It was truly one of the most spectacular locations for a city he'd ever seen. The high mountain peaks of Pilatus, and Rigi farther off, accompanied by several other majestic hills surrounding the city, provided epic views from nearly every angle.

"Whoever the original settlers of this town were sure could pick the spots," Sean commented dryly.

"Indeed," Emily agreed. "You snored a little," she jabbed changing the subject.

"Did I?" He sounded embarrassed, but she knew better.

"Yeah, but that's good. Means you were tired and needed the rest."

He nodded. "Yeah, I'm starting to remember why I got out of all this running around the world crap."

"One day back on the job and you're already complaining again?" she continued her attack.

"No. And I've been working for the last week, just so you know." He tried to add a smattering of being insulted to his defense, but it had no effect on the director.

"I'm just giving you a hard time, Agent Zero." She twisted her head toward him and winked. He didn't respond, instead shaking his head and looking out the window again.

She navigated the traffic lights and around the Reuss River that wound its way through the middle of the bustling city. People filled the cafes, restaurants, coffee shops, and boutiques lining the side-walks along the riverfront. The famous Chapel Bridge spanned the river. It was one of the largest covered wooden footbridges in the world. Next to it, founded in the rushing water, was a hexagonal stone chapel.

The bridge suffered a great deal of damage in 1993 when a fire destroyed many of the old paintings that hung from the bridge's ceiling, but the structure itself remained intact, and renovation efforts had it looking like brand new. Red and white flowers lined the bridge's railing in long, wooden flower boxes.

Emily drove the car past the bridge and into the business center of the city. Banks seemed to occupy every corner in the downtown district, a symbol of Switzerland's dominance in the world of finance. Next to them, appropriately, were several jewelry stores and high-end clothiers, along with a few fancier restaurants.

Just past the center of town, Emily found a parking spot outside a tall, gray apartment building. A flat metal awning extended out over the entryway.

"This is Dr. Ott's apartment," Emily said. "And it's where I have to drop you off."

She handed Sean a key and a Post-it Note with a number on it.

"That is the key to Ott's apartment, and the apartment number. Take a look around, and see if you can find anything."

"I'm sure the local police have already done a thorough job of screwing the place up."

"Probably. But it doesn't mean you shouldn't try. It's the first place we should look. Maybe you'll get lucky and find a lead."

He had a precarious look on his face. "And if I don't?"

She shrugged. "Then we'll have to try another angle. For now, though, we don't have another angle. Let me know if you find anything. But keep communication to a minimum. Same protocol as before. You're pretty much on your own with this."

He gave a solemn nod. "Understood."

Sean opened the door and got out, and she exited the driver's side. He stood on the sidewalk for a second and took inventory of his surroundings. A busy coffee shop across the street served a few dozen people inside and six or seven on the streetside tables. A music store, a shop that sold women's clothing, a bakery, and another bank rounded out the opposite side of the road's buildings. He scanned the faces of the passersby, but no one seemed to be paying him any mind.

Emily hit the remote lock on the keys and tossed them over to Sean. He snatched them out of the air and glanced at her questioningly.

"I've got another ride," she said. A second later, a silver BMW of the same make zipped around the corner and stopped on the street. "This one doesn't belong to us," she said, pointing at the black sedan. "So don't be too rough on it." She thought about it for a second and changed her mind. "On second thought, go nuts."

Emily opened the passenger door to the silver car and got in.

He didn't say goodbye to his friend, instead closing the door and turning around to face the apartment building. The BMW's engine revved, and the driver whipped the car back into traffic. Sean watched as the car disappeared around the corner, turning right to loop around and head back toward Germany.

At least he wouldn't have to find a ride if he needed one. Even though it was late spring and sunny, the temperature was fairly cool, for which Sean was grateful since it meant he could wear a jacket and a shoulder holster for his pistol. Despite having a license to kill, he preferred not to telegraph the fact that he was armed to the entire populace of Switzerland. He'd rather not do that anywhere he went, but certain countries had a skeptical view of carrying weapons. The irony was that Switzerland had a stellar reputation for making quality guns.

He zipped up his black jacket a little tighter and headed for the apartment complex entrance.

Inside the metal-and-glass entrance, he found a wide foyer with black and white tiles lining the floor. Two sets of elevators were at the far end. To the right, a wall full of bronze mailboxes nestled between a few fake plants in what he assumed were fake Ming-style vases resting on the floor.

He glanced back down at the piece of paper in his hand: #529. Clutching the key in the same hand, he walked steadily over to the elevator and hit the call button. A second later, the doors to his left opened, and he pressed the button for the fifth floor.

The elevator ride was short. When the doors opened again, he found himself in a hallway that extended to the left and right. A sign with two arrows directed visitors as to which way each apartment grouping was located. The one he was looking for was to the right.

He made his way down the hallway. Silver light fixtures with matted glass cast a pale glow into the hall, combined with the sunlight from windows at each end. Sean counted the numbers until he reached the one marked 529. He slid the key into the lock and turned it cautiously. There had been situations in the past where other agents had barged into a locked room only to find a hit squad waiting for them. Sometimes, it wasn't as obvious as an unlocked door or evidence of forced entry. Sometimes, villains were clever. As he eased the door open, he simultaneously drew his pistol. This version of his Springfield XD was compact, with a lengthened grip on the clip for better stabilization. With no silencer attached, he prayed silently that he wouldn't have to use it. Firing a weapon like that in close quarters could do severe long-term damage to human hearing.

Sean shook off the random thoughts. *Stay focused,* he told himself. He led with his pistol, keeping it out in front as he pushed across the threshold. Inside, he found something he hadn't really expected. The apartment was in good order. The black couch was pressed neatly against the wall. A small metal writing desk with a glass top sat next to it. A few documents lay on top, but the rest of the letters and other paperwork were organized and placed in slots on a shelf that ran along the back edge. Either whoever kidnapped Dr. Ott was mindful enough to put everything back where they found it, or the police screwed up the scene.

It looked as if no one had searched the place, though. As he recalled the information Emily had given him, that notion actually made sense. She'd said that Ott was taken while at her research laboratory. That meant the Black Ring might not have even come here. Why would they? If they had Ott, they wouldn't need anything from here.

He closed the door behind him, making sure to lock it again just in case someone was following. To the left was a small bathroom. It was minimally decorated, white walls and tiles, an ordinary glass shower, and a small washer and dryer next to the sink. He crept deeper into the apartment, keeping his weapon drawn and ready. Around the entryway corner, he found a small kitchen with white, Swedish-modern cabinetry, a matching white bistro table with two chairs and a stainless refrigerator. Through a pair of double doors, a balcony opened up with a view of downtown Lucerne. Through some of the canyons of buildings, he could get a peek at sections of the Reuss River.

A loud clicking sound came from a room off to the right of the living room. Sean raised his gun and aimed it through an open doorway. He could see the corner of a bed on the other side. Light poured into the bedroom from a window that was out of his line of sight. But in the light, he noticed a shadow moving around.

He stepped cautiously, careful not to make a noise on the faux wood flooring as he approached the bedroom door. He heard the noise again. It sounded like someone rummaging around just around the corner of the bedroom. When he reached the doorframe, he paused for a second, forcing himself to breathe calmly. Then he whipped the pistol around the corner and checked every corner of the room within two seconds. He saw what was causing the noise and lowered his gun. A pigeon was occasionally tapping on the window with its wings as the bird fluttered them.

Sean sighed. "Stupid bird," he said to himself.

The bedroom was as simply decorated as the rest of the home. A flat black floor bed sat low in the center of the room against the back wall. The sheets were plain white. A few black-and-white paintings hung on the wall across from the footboard. Another bathroom, the master, was situated through a narrow doorway to the left. Across from it was a small closet.

"It's like looking at the IKEA catalogue in here," he muttered.

Although one thing did seem out of place: Next to a black dresser, a wooden desk sat at an angle in the corner. It didn't match any of the other decor, and was clearly much older than everything else in the place. It had a main drawer and two lower drawers on either side of the sitting area.

Keeping his weapon low, but still at the ready, Sean walked over to the bathroom and checked inside, then checked the closet, just in case. Both were clear. He shoved the weapon back in its holster and walked back to the living room. He flipped open a black organizer and searched through some of the entries. Most of Dr. Ott's calendar was open, save for a few meetings she'd written down with other doctors. They must have been research scientists like her.

He closed the organizer and started sifting through some of the other papers and letters on the desk. There were utility bills, a medical bill for a routine checkup, a few pieces of correspondence for new credit cards, and a subscription renewal form for a scientific journal he'd never heard of.

None of it was helpful.

Sean walked over to the kitchen and searched through the drawers, pulling them out one at a time. Again he found nothing, only silverware, a typical kitchen drawer full of scissors, pens and tape, and one with a few hand towels in it.

He rubbed his eyes for a moment then pinched his nose. "What were you working on, Dr. Ott, that got you into so much trouble?"

His voice bounced around the room, but the walls had no answer.

Sean walked back into the bedroom and over to the dresser. He felt a little odd about going through a strange woman's personal things, but if she'd hidden something there, he needed to find it.

Panties and socks filled the top drawer, which he quickly closed when he realized there was nothing else in there. The second drawer proved equally embarrassing for him and just as disappointing. All he could find were brassieres, pantyhose, and a few more items of underwear that were a little more risqué.

He shook his head as he closed the second drawer. "Sorry, Dr. Ott," he said quietly.

The contents of the lower two drawers were less personal, jeans and T-shirts for the most part. But still, nothing of interest in regard to why the Black Ring would have taken the scientist.

Sean scratched his head. It was one of the most sterile scenes he'd ever investigated. Not a single clue as to what Dr. Ott had been working on or why she'd been kidnapped. The next place he'd need to look would be the research lab. That would be information he'd need to get from the report Emily had emailed him.

He started to take out his phone to check the email when he remembered he'd not checked the antique desk in the corner. He took a few steps over to it and pulled the matching chair out from under the seating spot. He sat down and tugged on the middle drawer. Inside were old black-and-white photos of people he didn't recognize, probably some of her old relatives. From the clothes they wore, it appeared that the pictures were probably taken around the 1930s or early 40s. There was a young man with dark hair and round spectacles with a woman of roughly the same age. In some of the pictures, the man was in a white lab coat. There were a few of the couple together, including one that must have been their wedding day.

Sean closed the center drawer and opened the one on the left. It contained various files, most of them empty, but a few that held sheets with mathematical equations he didn't understand scribbled on them. He pushed that drawer closed and opened the one on the right. There were a few books stacked inside. The *Bible* was on top of two others, a book on physics, and another on the science of black holes. Again, though, nothing that would be of help in the current situation.

He gently placed the books back in the drawer and started to close it when he noticed something odd. His eyes narrowed and he reached back over to the other drawer, twisting in the chair, and opened it again. His gaze shifted from one drawer to the other and back again, comparing the two with a critical eye. There was definitely something different about the drawer on the right. The back of it was a good four to six inches shallower at the back than the one on the left.

He leaned over and yanked on the back of the drawer. It was loose, and after a few more pulls, he was able to free the false back from its housing. Wedged into the small space in the rear of the drawer was a small leather notebook. Sean plucked it from its hiding spot and placed it on the desktop. The cover had been well worn with time, indicating that it was at least several decades old. The other thing that indicated how old the book might be was a familiar symbol pressed into the cover: a Nazi swastika.

Sean frowned at the emblem, more out of confusion than disdain. "Dr. Ott is a Nazi?" he mumbled the words.

The bird at the window flapped its wings again, startling Sean once more. He returned his attention to the leather book but was slow to open it, like a medieval monk peering into an ancient tome of holy scripture. Inside were more of the strange calculations he'd seen on some of the other papers he'd examined, but these had pictures accompanying them.

"I really should have taken calculus," he whispered as he pored over the strange drawings and detailed formulas.

The initial drawings in the book featured something that looked like a metal cube. The detail was fairly strong, right down to the rivets holding the box together; an open door on the side revealed a chair and what looked like a control panel. The date at the top of the page read, *17/04/1942.*

With wide eyes, Sean flipped the pages, finding more drawings, math, and notations written in German. While he struggled with the high-level math, he could read the German almost fluently. The notes, however, were talking about tests they'd run with powerful magnets. Through the first several pages, the experiments had been unsuccessful.

As Sean turned each page, he noticed that the designs of the box changed. Initially, it had been a cube, but as the journal entry dates progressed, it became more rounded.

He continued to pour over the pages, absorbing the information as fast as he could.

"What were you up to?" he asked aloud.

One of the last drawings in the book featured an image that was nothing like the one at the beginning. The object had mutated from a metal cube to something that looked more like a bell. There were people standing around, staring at it from below. It had been anchored, Sean assumed with chains, to several pillars that stood in a circle. What he couldn't figure out was the thing that hovered over the bell. It looked like a swirling hole, but the artist had left a little too much to the imagination, and the author's description was vague at best.

The next to last entry was dated *08/04/1945* and proclaimed the experiment to be a success, and that only a little more testing would be necessary before they attempted to use the device with a human subject.

On the final page, no date was given, and the writing had changed somewhat. It appeared to be sloppier, as if written in a hurry. The context of the words gave a clue as to why.

The Nazis were so close to achieving their goal. I managed to steer their scientists with incorrect assumptions and calculations for the last three years, which I pray was long enough to keep them from success. The Allies are closing in around them, and it will not be long before they are defeated. Die Glocke has been removed from its housings and was put on a train bound for Hamburg. I overheard some of the soldiers saying the device would be taken to South America, where several of the high command were rumored to go if the war was lost.

I pray the help of Saint Sebastian in this endeavor.

"Die Glocke?" he said aloud. That would require a little digging, but for now, he wanted to get out of Dr. Ott's apartment to somewhere a little more neutral. One of the many coffee shops he'd seen on the way in came to mind. He'd be able to access the Internet faster and have some privacy by blending in with the crowds of patrons. Sean grabbed the little book and stuffed it in his rucksack.

He stood up and started for the door when he heard the clicking again. He turned his head to the window, but the bird was gone. Sean froze in place near the bedroom door and leaned back against the wall. The sound came from the living room. The second time around, he recognized the noise. It was the sound of someone manipulating the lock.

6

Lucerne, Switzerland

Sean pressed his back against the wall and waited. Someone was trying to get into the apartment. It could have been the local authorities, but he doubted it. They would have got a key from the apartment manager. Even if it was the police, Sean knew that wasn't much better. If they found him in here, his mission would be compromised before it even began. At best, it would put him several hours behind the clock, and he was already fighting the time issue.

Whoever was at the door was attempting to pick it, which meant they were potentially hostile. He pulled the weapon out of its holster, holding it near his face and keeping his shoulder dug into the doorframe. In an instant, he remembered the balcony. Part of it stretched around behind part of the wall, which would give him a temporary hiding place. Of course, if whoever was at the door happened to walk over to the balcony doors, he'd be exposed.

It was his only option.

Sean padded hurriedly across the floor like a 180-pound mouse. He turned the latch on the balcony door, but it wouldn't budge. His heart pounded, but he forced himself to remain calm. He looked down and realized it was locked. *Why would someone lock a door five stories up?* He twisted the lock and tugged on the latch, slipping outside as he heard the lock on the front door give way.

He pulled the balcony door closed as quietly as possible and slipped around the edge of the wall just as he saw the front open. All he'd seen was a gloved hand coming around the corner at the front, reaffirming what he'd believed about the intruder. The realization of his current situation struck him after a few seconds of standing on the balcony. Since he could remember, Sean had been afraid of heights, a phobia that had plagued him throughout his entire life. People had suggested he see a therapist about it, but he was always too busy for anything like that. The oddity behind his fear was that, as a boy, he'd climbed trees all the time, never fearing falling or getting hurt. But buildings and high mountains were a different animal altogether. Even at the less-extreme height of five stories, his heart dropped into his stomach.

He pressed his back against the wall, still clutching his weapon with one hand but pushing hard against the smooth, brushed steel siding with the other. He could hear the intruder rummaging through some things inside. From the sound of it, the person was probably in the living room, knocking over the desk, shelving, and some of the other things in the area. *These guys are a little late to the party,* Sean thought, distracting himself for a moment from the dizzying heights.

His mind returned to it, though, as he realized he needed to get out of there.

To his right, the next-door balcony presented his only option. He shuffled his feet, inch by inch, until he reached the railing. The distance between the two porches was temptingly close. Maybe five feet. To him, it looked more like twenty. For two seconds, he briefly considered the possibility that whoever was inside the apartment might actually not check the balcony. Why would they? Surely, what-ever they were looking for wouldn't be out there? Would it?

He shrugged off the thoughts. The intruder didn't need a reason to check the balcony. Sheer curiosity would be enough to catch Sean, at which point he would have to shoot his way out, something he'd rather not do in the current environment. Then again, he'd rather not try to jump five feet from one railing to another.

A horrible sequence of visions flashed through his head. One of them involved losing his footing and completely missing the jump, followed by his body plummeting to the pavement below next to a stream of pedestrians. He took a deep breath and swallowed hard. There was no other option. He had to get away clean, and this was the only way.

He tucked his gun back into the holster and snapped the button on the strap to hold it in place. His breathing quickened as he lifted his leg up over the rail and straddled it for a moment before putting his foot on the narrow, metal beam. Fortunately, the top of the rail was flat, giving him at least a small edge on which to balance. He picked up his other foot and stood erect, keeping his balance and most of his weight on his right hand as it pressed against the wall. He fought the urge to look down, but his peripheral vision saw everything else: the city skyline, the cars moving slowly through traffic, and yes, the five-story fall. A gust of wind whipped up, seemingly out of nowhere, and nearly caused him to lose his balance. He shifted his weight slightly, steadying himself against the heavy breeze.

Sean took in one more long, slow breath. "You got this," he muttered to himself. He bent both knees and pushed off hard, but his left foot slipped and didn't give an optimal boost. He hurtled at an awkward angle through the air, but his jump was much shorter than necessary. His hands shot up instinctively in an attempt to grab the other balcony, but his fingertips scraped the edge as he flew past. A sickening sensation filled Sean's mind. The gushing air underneath him sent a chill through his spine as he fell. His fears had come true. He winced for a second, knowing that the thing he'd been afraid of his entire life had finally come to fruition.

All of this ran through his mind in the span of two seconds. The third second, he realized he was heading for the balcony directly below the one he'd aimed for. His body hurtled to the concrete platform. He put his feet out and hit with the left foot first, then the right, and let his lower body go limp, falling to the hard landing with a roll. His back hit the railing on the other side of the balcony, stopping him cold.

Sean looked around for a second and realized he was okay. His back throbbed a little from hitting the rail right where the man in Agadir had struck him with his elbow, but other than that, he was fine.

Better lucky than good, he thought. But he wasn't out of the woods yet.

He forced himself back onto his feet and over to the balcony door. He put his hand on the latch and prayed silently that these tenants weren't as paranoid as Dr. Ott. He twisted the aluminum latch and was relieved that it gave way. He poked his head inside and looked around. The layout to the apartment was a replica of the one upstairs. The decor, however, was much different.

Pictures of cats adorned the walls. An afghan was hung over a couch that looked like it was something left over from the early 1980s. The kitchen cabinets were the same as upstairs, telling him that the contractor had provided the same to every unit.

Sean listened for a second. He didn't see anyone, but that didn't mean no one was home. Quietly, he stepped into the home and eased the door shut. He didn't hear anything. He hurried over to the door, opened it, and exited the apartment. The elevators were close by, but he opted for taking the stairs. If the man searching through the apartment upstairs had finished and was coming down, being on the elevator with him would be awkward, like messy awkward, which Sean hoped to avoid as much as possible. He'd already made a mess at the hotel in Morocco. He'd promised himself he wouldn't leave a huge body count everywhere he went if it could be helped, in spite of the fact that the nature of some of his future missions might require it.

He arrived at the end of the hallway and pushed through the stairwell door. His eyes shot up and then down to make sure no one was in there like the day before in Agadir. It was clear, and he rushed down the stairs. Fluorescent lights lining the underside of the stairs made it easy for him to see as he descended.

When he reached the bottom, Sean slowed his pace as he entered the building's lobby. He scanned the room as he walked quickly from the back of the facility to the entrance/exit. A blonde woman was grabbing mail from one of the bronze boxes on the far left wall, but other than that, the lobby was empty.

He pushed through the front door and walked out onto the street. The fresh air filled his lungs again, mingled with a slight hint of car exhaust, bread from the bakery across the street, and a waft of coffee.

He'd planned to do some research at the coffee shop, but now the plan had changed.

With a quick check in both directions to make sure no cars were coming, Sean sprinted across the road, through a small black fenced gate on the other side, and slowed as he entered the coffee shop. He found a seat at one of the tinted windows and pretended to look through it.

A frail-looking brunette girl with a brown apron and white button-up shirt came over to where he was sitting.

She asked him in German if he would like something to drink.

He replied fluently in a polite but curt tone, ordering a cappuccino.

She smiled at him as she walked away, making a note of his order.

He didn't care about the drink. All Sean needed was the seat with a view of the apartment complex. Someone had left a newspaper on the counter next to him. He picked it up and pretended to read the business section, keeping the paper over the bottom half of his face. He peered over the top of it, intensely watching the apartment build-ing's front doors.

The girl returned in less than four minutes with his drink. "Danke," he said the German word for thank you and offered her a grateful smile.

She blushed a little and nodded before slinking back to the coffee bar.

Sean didn't let her see him roll his eyes. She was half his age. Maybe. It was hard to tell anymore.

He took a small sip of the milk and espresso and continued to focus on the building across the way.

Five more minutes and half the cappuccino later, Sean saw the man appear through the entrance. He'd not seen the face before, and now he wasn't wearing gloves, but the man's red shirtsleeve had been visible when entering Dr. Ott's unit, and that was enough for Sean. Now the guy stuck out like a sore thumb. His hair was dark with thick waves. He had the stern face of someone who rarely found humor in things, and a thin layer of stubble from ear to ear.

The man looked in both directions as he stepped onto the street. He appeared to be looking for something or someone. He turned and started walking to the right, heading back toward the center of town. Sean took another sip of his coffee, left enough euros on the counter to cover his tab and a small tip and walked out.

Sean stayed on the opposite side of the street to the man he was following. While he was in pursuit, he decided it would be a good opportunity to multitask. If he was on the phone, it would disguise his presence slightly in case the man knew who Sean was and what he was up to. Plus, it would give Sean a chance to get the ball rolling on the research side of things.

He slid the phone out of his pocket and flipped through a few of his recent calls, finding the ID he was looking for he hit the green *call* button.

A few rings later, a man on the other end answered. "Well, well, well. If it isn't the amazing Sean Wyatt."

"Listen, Tommy. I have something I need you to look into." He cut through the niceties and went straight to business.

"Okay, buddy. Everything all right?"

"At the moment. I'm trying to find some information on a Nazi experiment. I think the device they were constructing was called *die Glocke.*"

"Die Glocke?" Tommy made sure he'd heard correctly.

"Yeah. It's German."

"I figured that when you said the word, *Nazi*."

"Right." Sean shook his head.

"You sound out of breath."

Sean was breathing hard, though it wasn't from the pace of his pursuit. He was walking fast, but he was trying to focus on not losing his quarry. It was the intensity of the chase that caused him to take in short bursts of air.

"I'm fine. Just walking through Lucerne at the moment. The air is a little thinner up here."

"Lucerne?" Tommy sounded surprised. "What are you doing there? I love that city. One time--"

Sean cut him off. "Tommy, I need you to pay attention. Find out all you can about die Glocke, and any information on a man with the last name of Ott. I think he was a scientist that was working for the Nazis on the project. Get me all you can about those things."

The other end of the line was silent for a moment as Tommy was jotting down everything his friend had requested. Tommy Schultz was the head of the IAA based in Atlanta. He and his younger assistants, Alex and Tara, were bloodhounds when it came to digging up facts on just about anything.

If there was any information out there on the older Ott and the device known as die Glocke, Tommy and his crew would find it.

"Okay, I think I got it. Anything else you want me to look up? An itemized list of priceless art stolen by the Nazis?" His tone was sarcastic despite the fact that he was being helpful.

"No, maybe later," Sean cracked. Then "Wait. See what you can find out about a Nazi U-boat heading to South America. I want to know if there is any documentation about transporting technology or anything else across the Atlantic in one of their subs."

"Well, that could be tricky," Tommy said.

"Because?"

"For starters, the idea of Nazi leaders escaping the Fatherland to South America, particularly Argentina, isn't a new theory. In most circles, it's a widely held belief that many U-boats did, in fact, make the journey across the ocean successfully."

"Good. Then we are dealing with facts and not myth. See what you can find."

Tommy sighed. "Fine. But it's not like I'm just sitting around watching television here. I do work, you know."

"This is more important, Tommy. Thanks for your help."

"You're..."

Sean ended the call before he could hear the word *welcome*. He imagined his friend cursing on the other end, but he didn't care. The idea made Sean grin for a second. Then the man he was following ducked around the corner steps of a bank, disappearing behind the metal façade. Sean glanced both ways and darted across the street in pursuit.

"Now where are you going?" he whispered.

7

Washington, D.C.

Admiral McClain stood at his second-story window overlooking the Potomac River. He considered all the history that had taken place on that little strip of water as he puffed on a Padrón cigar. One of the first things that came to mind was the famous crossing of George Washington. The painting had become an icon in Revolutionary lore, but from what he understood about the real history of it, things didn't exactly go down that way. Not that it mattered. The fledgling country persevered, and was able to break the bonds that the British had kept them in for so long.

McClain had joined the armed services because he wanted to be a part of the great military history of the United States of America. He hoped to carve out his own little piece that generations would admire.

It hadn't gone according to plan, though.

Some would look at McClain's status and all his achievements in life and think he had it all, that he'd done everything he set out to do. They'd be right. Mostly.

But Corbett McClain wanted more. It wasn't enough that he was one of the chief advisers to the president. He snorted at the thought. Earlier that morning, the president had taken action in spite of McClain's advice. He felt more like a pawn now than ever.

He'd achieved the highest rank for a naval officer, but was still unsatisfied with his standing, as well as his paycheck. He wasn't living in squalor by any stretch of the imagination. His multimillion-dollar home on the river put to rest any notion of the sort. He drove a modest luxury car, smoked the best cigars, drank the best bourbon, and when his wife was out of town, probably engaging in one of her many extramarital affairs, he had a stable of women he paid to keep him company.

Life was good. But it wasn't what he wanted.

McClain took another draw on his cigar and let the bluish smoke seep out between his pursed lips.

It wasn't enough that McClain was one of the right hands to the most powerful man on the planet. He wanted recognition. He wanted to be a hero. And despite his finances, he wanted...no, needed, more money.

The president should have listened about the SEALs. He could send those guys in to do anything, and they would take care of it before the deadline. The missing scientist would be saved, and McClain would be the guy responsible for heading the rescue mission. Well, maybe not heading, but at least ordering it.

His phone rattled on a nearby end table as it vibrated. He stepped over and picked it up. Recognizing the number, he answered shortly, "What?"

"Still waiting on your orders, sir."

"So? Keep waiting. I'll let you know when it's time to move. We don't even know where to move to, yet."

"I understand that, sir. But usually in these situations, it's best not to sit around and wait. You know that."

"I do." He paused and momentarily changed the subject. "Were you able to find any information yet?"

"Not yet, sir. We have a few men on it, but so far they're coming up empty. I'm not sure there's anything out there that will help."

"It's out there," McClain reassured the caller. "You just have to know where to look. You already tried Ott's lab?"

"Yeah, but it was hard to get in there. They've tightened security considerably."

"Getting past tight security is one of the reasons you're a part of this unit. We need to know what she's got. There has to be something that can point us in the right direction."

"I'll take care of it, sir."

"That's more like it. Call me when you have an update on the situation."

"Yes, sir. One more thing you should know about. There's an asset in play."

It wasn't exactly news. The president had so much as already told McClain that there would be an Axis agent on the scene. Still, the wild card presented an opportunity.

"Follow him, and see where he goes, what he's up to. If he finds something helpful, let me know."

"Will do."

McClain ended the call. "What are you up to?" he said to himself in a gruff tone. Knowing Sean Wyatt's history, he knew the man could get in the way of his plan. But there was no turning back now. Things were in motion, and they couldn't be stopped just because some cowboy was getting in the way.

Hopefully, by the end of the day, he would have some answers — answers that could lead to taking some action.

8

Lucerne, Switzerland

Sean kept a few hundred feet between himself and the guy in the red shirt. The man had been walking for over ten minutes, winding his way through the streets of the city. The longer he followed him, the more Sean started to think that either the guy was an ordinary criminal, or he was trying to lead Sean astray. The latter became increasingly the more likely.

He checked his six more frequently as the minutes rolled by, making sure no one was on his tail. A few times he thought he recognized the same guy behind him, but when he would look again, the person was gone, never to reappear.

Red shirt took a sharp right and cut down an alleyway between two buildings. If Sean followed, he would definitely be spotted. He had to risk guessing where his mark was headed.

Up ahead, the street ended in a sharp left turn. Straight ahead was the river. To the right was a pedestrian street with cafes and restaurants along the waterfront. He was back to an area he recognized. Red shirt's direction would take him out in the middle of the waterfront area. Sean sped up to a jog, weaving around the citizens and tourists as he increased his pace. He needed to get to the other side of the row of buildings before his quarry disappeared.

It was another thirty seconds before Sean reached the intersection and the entrance to the pedestrian street. When he got there, though, he let out a deep sigh. Hundreds of people milled about the area. A few Asian visitors were getting their picture taken near the entrance to the wooden footbridge. A hodgepodge of other people stood outside the cafes, sat at tables, drinking wine and beer or eating their lunches while others just seemed to be walking aimlessly around as they enjoyed the sights.

He'd lost the man in the red shirt.

Sean started making his way through the glut of people, edging his way past shoulders, fanny packs, and backpacks. Up ahead, he saw hair that looked exactly like the guy he was chasing. Sean picked up the pace again and attempted to hurry through the throng.

He nearly caught up with the man, getting as close as thirty feet away. But the mark turned and started walking in the other direction. When he did, Sean noticed the guy had on a green shirt. He'd spotted the wrong guy.

Sean spun around on his heels, searching the crowd for the apartment intruder, but he was nowhere to be found. "Good job, Sean. Lost a lead," he cursed himself.

He took a long, slow breath. "Where did you go?"

After a minute of looking around without success, he stepped out of the flow of traffic and stood next to one of the decorative black fences that surrounded an Italian restaurant. He glanced at the menu. The description of the different dishes sounded delicious, and he was starting to get hungry. As he tried to decide what to do, his stomach grumbled, giving him the sign he was looking for.

At the very least, he figured he could sit outside and wait to see if red shirt happened to come by again. If the man doubled back, Sean would be there ready for him.

He stepped over to the hostess stand where a short, young woman with straight brown hair down to her shoulders awaited in a black button-up shirt and matching pants.

"A table for one, please," he said in nearly perfect German. "Outside if possible." He passed her a warm grin.

She smiled at him and grabbed a menu from one of the pulpit's shelves. "Right this way."

Sean sat with his back to the restaurant so he could face the water and keep an eye on the faces that walked by. He decided to get spaghetti with meatballs and a salad. The lasagna looked amazing, but eating something heavy like that when he was on a mission was something Sean rarely did. He liked to keep light so he could stay on his toes.

The server brought him a glass of water with no ice, and he drank it quickly, not realizing how thirsty he'd got from his activities thus far.

Sean studied the people as they passed by. After ten minutes, his plate of food arrived with the salad on the side. He thanked the server and dug into the pasta, devouring it in only a few minutes. The robust, red spaghetti sauce had a sharp garlic flavor to it, along with potent Italian herbs. The meatballs were hearty, seasoned with onions, garlic, and pepper. He made quick work of the salad as well, and gnawed on a few pieces of bread that came with the meal.

Another twenty minutes went by without ever seeing the man in the red shirt again. Sean was mad at himself for losing the guy, but being angry wouldn't help anything.

He remembered the book he'd put in his rucksack and took it out, careful not to let anyone see the swastika on the front. His fingers flipped through the pages again, and he read some of the notes that the older Ott had made:

If the Führer were to succeed with these experiments, it could alter the course of history and the future.

Sean wondered what the device was capable of doing. He recalled what he'd been told so far, and what the book said. Things were still fairly vague. He needed answers, and fast. Time was running out for Dr. Ott.

He took his phone out of his pocket to see if anyone had called. It was a little surprising that there'd been no word from Tommy, even though it had only been about thirty minutes since he'd talked to his friend. Tommy worked fast, and his two assistants were always ready for a little sleuthing.

Might as well do some research himself while he was waiting. There wasn't anything else to do.

He tapped on the app for his favorite search engine and typed in the words *die glocke*. After a few seconds, several links appeared on the first page. One featured a video. Others were links to websites containing information on the subject. His eyebrows furrowed as he frowned and clicked on one of the blue links. "How is it that so many people know what this thing is, and I've never heard of it?" he wondered aloud.

The website appeared on his screen, and he started reading about the odd device the Nazis had tried to develop. Most of what he was seeing was conjecture. Some people believed that die Glocke was some kind of a UFO that Hitler had created in order to spread his would-be Aryan nation throughout the cosmos. Other theories stated that the device was designed as a means of time travel. One of the more interesting ideas Sean noted was the notion that die Glocke could manipulate space-time, creating a wormhole around itself and essentially disappearing from the current dimension.

According to the website, the tests for the device happened at a place called Der Riese near the Wenceslas mine in Poland, fairly close to the Czech border. The story suggested that the Third Reich murdered many of the scientists working on the project when things began to go south for the Germans. Apparently, they didn't want anyone sharing their research or any findings with the enemy.

In the text, Sean noticed mention of something called, *"The Henge,"* which was described as a circle of concrete columns that may have been used to anchor the device. He held the book down and flipped to the page where he remembered seeing something similar to that description. Sure enough, the more Sean looked at it, the more the circle looked like a kind of Stonehenge. *But why?*

He did a quick search for the location of the Wenceslaus mine and set a waypoint on his phone's map. After putting the book back in his rucksack, he got up from the table and started walking back to the car he'd left in front of Ott's apartment building.

It took nearly fifteen minutes for him to get back to the sedan. He hadn't realized how far the guy in the red shirt had taken him through the city when he was in pursuit.

Sean opened the vehicle and set the rucksack in the back seat. He slid into the driver's seat and adjusted the settings before firing up the engine. Sean wasn't a car guy. He loved motorcycles and had a small museum's worth of them back in Atlanta. Often people asked him if he just collected bikes or if he actually rode them. He found the question to be annoying, but always responded by telling people the only reason to own a motorcycle is to ride it. He didn't have them on display for the public or anything like that. They were kept in a safe place, in his massive garage below the house.

But even a motorcycle guy could appreciate the sound of the BMW's motor as it revved to life. It brought a subtle grin to his face as he gripped the wheel and shifted into drive.

He was stopped before he could take off. The familiar vibration of his phone going off in his pocket caused him to shift the car back into park, killing the momentary thrill of anticipation.

"What have you got, Tommy?"

"I'm doing fine, thanks. Weather here in Atlanta is awesome right now."

Sean shook his head and briefly considered hanging up on his friend, except that he loved the smart aleck response. "Great. Good to know. Tell me something."

"We're still researching the submarine thing. That might take a while, but there are some promising angles the kids are looking into. As far as die Glocke is concerned, you could have done an Internet search to find out some interesting things about that. "

Sean snorted but tried not to be demeaning. "Already did that, buddy. I'm headed to Poland right now to see what I can find."

"Oh, good. So you were just going to drive out to Poland to see what you could find? It's not that small of a country, you know."

Tommy was laying on the cynicism pretty thick. It was a staple in their friendship.

"No, smart guy. I have a general location. The area near the Czech border where there's a mine. I figured I'd check it out."

"That's not bad. But I can go you one better."

"Impress me."

"I've got a name for you. Michel Steiner."

Sean waited for his friend to continue, but Tommy was apparently going to make him ask. "Okay, who is that?"

"Glad you asked," Tommy said dryly. "He is the son of one of the soldiers that worked on the project with Dr. Ott's grandfather. He runs a nonprofit organization that his father founded. It has something to do with helping people find jobs, like a temp agency. If anyone knows something about what they were working on and what might have happened to die Glocke, it would be him. He's the only direct link to the project we can find, aside from Dr. Ott of course."

A few seconds passed in silence. Sean considered what his friend had just told him. "Well, I am definitely impressed," he said finally. "Not sure how you were able to get that little nugget so quickly, but something tells me you didn't do it on your own."

"That would be a correct assumption. Alex and Tara were all over it. It turns out that Steiner has come out with several books on the subject of die Glocke, so finding him wasn't all that difficult." There was a hint of hesitation before Tommy continued. "I do have to warn you, though. From what we were able to find, this guy sounds a little...how should I say...eccentric?"

There was the rub Sean had been waiting for. "Great. So you're sending me to talk to some nut job conspiracy theorist?"

"Now hold on. It's not entirely like that. He does have some credibility, and there's no denying he's the son of someone that worked on that project."

"No denying?"

"Well, I mean it's possible that he's completely full of it, but he's the only lead we have. And not many people would come out of the woodwork and admit that their father had been part of the SS.

Although his father *was* a defector. He ran away from the army because he didn't believe in the Third Reich's mission. Again, that's what Michel has told people. He's probably got some documents or something to corroborate that part of the story."

Sean's heart sank. Tommy had got his hopes up that this case just got easier, but now it was back down to earth. "Let me get this straight. You're basing your information on what this guy claims and nothing else?"

"More or less," Tommy said then quickly pressed on. "But even if he's some crackpot, he might have more information on the subject than anyone else simply due to proximity and from what he's studied."

Finally, a valid point.

"Okay," Sean said reluctantly. "What's his address?"

"I'm texting it to you right now. Definitely give this guy a chance, at least. He might be able to help, and he seems like a nice person. Anyone who donates their time to a charitable operation can't be all bad."

It didn't mean he'd be helpful either, but it was all they had to go on. "All right, Tommy. Thanks. I'm headed that way now. I'll be in touch if I need anything else. And let me know if you find out something on that sub."

"Will do."

Sean hung up the phone and steered the car out into the traffic. His mind wandered, riddled with doubts and concern. *Wild goose chase. Going to meet a crazy person in Poland. Almost fell to my death earlier. Coming back was definitely the right decision.*

9

Miłków, Poland

Sean woke up to the first signs of daylight in a tiny bedroom. The dark wooden headboard and multicolored comforter reminded him of childhood nights spent at his grandparents' house. A matching mirror and dresser were opposite of the bed and a small, square window was the only view into the outside world. He rubbed his eyes and made his way to the shower in a haze.

The drive from Lucerne to the Polish border had not been a short one. When Sean arrived, it was nearly two in the morning, local time. He'd parked the car outside an inn and managed to stumble inside, exhausted from his travels.

During the last four hours of the drive, he'd struggled to keep the car on the lonely roads that wound through Germany, brushing by the Czech Republic, and across the border into Poland. The first part of the journey had been picturesque, filled with rolling foothills, the tall Harz Mountains in the distance, flat farmlands, lush forests, and the occasional city.

Somehow, he managed to find his way to the check in counter where a scraggly-haired woman with bad teeth and a fleshy face welcomed him to the inn. Sean was glad he'd been able to get a room, although what he'd seen of the town so far didn't exactly leave an impression on him as a touristy place. On the drive in, most of the village's lights were scattered about, reminding him more of a rural farming community than a city.

He took a ten-minute shower, letting the hot water soothe his skin and dull the effects of waking up so early. It was getting harder and harder for Sean to get a full night's sleep. Lately, the norm had been to get four to five hours at most. This morning had been no different, and the sleep he had been able to get was restless at best.

Visions of Dufort escaping and running amok somewhere in the world kept resurfacing. He wondered if Adriana was okay. And he worried a little about the missing scientist, Dr. Ott. He'd only seen pictures of her in the dossier Emily had sent. She seemed like a nice enough person from her image, but of course, he knew not to judge too soon. Even if she wasn't a terribly friendly person, she was at the very least innocent, and that warranted his help.

He got out of the shower and dried off, rubbed on a little deodorant, and slipped into one of two sets of clean clothes he had with him. He'd packed light so he could remain more mobile. But if this mission went more than a few days, he would need to buy some additional clothes — on the company card, of course.

He grinned at the thought of Emily seeing a bill from a clothier in Prague. She'd be furious, and that almost made him want to make the drive right then and there.

Sean slipped his shoes on and stuffed some of his loose things back into his bag. He slung the rucksack over one shoulder and the backpack over the other and walked to the lobby. A young man, probably in his midtwenties, had replaced the woman from the night before. He smiled brightly and said something to Sean in Polish. It was one of the languages he didn't speak.

"Sorry, I don't know Polish," he apologized.

"Not a problem, sir," the man said in perfect English. "I simply asked if you had a good night's rest."

"As good as I've had in a long time," Sean said. He wasn't lying.

The few hours of sleep he had were better than nothing, and he'd needed them badly.

"That's good to hear, sir. If you have any questions for me, don't hesitate to ask."

Sean thanked him and laid the key to his room on the counter, turned, and headed for the door. He hadn't paid much attention to the lobby the night before. He'd been so tired that the memory of even walking into the inn was a blank spot in his mind. Now he took in the quaint interior decor. Dark molding framed the windows, surrounded by dark yellow walls. Vibrant green plants occupied nearly every corner. He could see flower boxes outside the windows, filled with blooms of yellow, white, and purple. There was a sitting area with a sofa and a few chairs near a television. Off to the right, the early risers were getting their breakfast in a small cafeteria-like room.

He left the inn and stepped out into the fresh, warm morning air. According to the weather app on his phone, the local temperatures had been unseasonably hot so far. Nothing like what he was accustomed to in southern Tennessee and north Georgia, but warmer than expected.

He took in the surroundings in an instant, filling the void his mind had left vacant several hours earlier.

The little village only had a small main street that featured a few businesses. Of course, there was a baker and a butcher. It was one of the things Sean loved about Europe; every town seemed to have those two things. He glanced down at his phone and noted the location he was looking for. From the looks of it, the place where he could find Michel Steiner was only a block or so away.

Sean walked around the green hedgerow that separated the inn from the sidewalk and unconsciously remembered where he'd parked his car in a lot just to the left of the inn. He left his backpack in the trunk and headed at a brisk pace toward Steiner's office.

The town was a stark contrast to the busy city center of Lucerne. The Swiss town he'd just left was full of activity, traffic, citizens walking around all over the place, and a myriad of colors, smells, and sights. While the Polish countryside was every bit as beautiful, this small village sported only a few citizens strolling lazily about and seemingly even less automobile traffic. Sean met every face with a polite smile, which was returned by the passersby. It was a practice he'd started using more lately, figuring that a friendly person stuck out less than a person who was trying to look unmemorable.

After passing a stationery store, he found the building he was looking for on the other side of the street. He checked both directions and jogged across, gripping the rucksack with his right hand. Sean didn't understand what the lettering on the building's façade said, but the number matched the one he was given by Tommy.

He opened the glass door and walked inside. The room was empty except for a man who looked to be in his midsixties sitting behind a plain, black desk that looked like it was from the 1970s. It had a woodgrain Formica top and crooked legs. Sean was surprised it could actually support its own weight. A small waiting area with six chairs was next to the window. Sean walked through it and over to the desk. There were no identifying placards, but he assumed the man who was busily writing something on a sheet of paper was the guy he sought.

"Michel Steiner?" he said with an air of uncertainty.

"You sound like an American," the man said without looking up from his notepad. Whatever he was working on must have been important, in spite of the lack of people waiting to be served.

His thin, white hair gave way to a few age spots on his scalp. Sean couldn't see his eyes, but the man was wearing thin, wireframe glasses, a light-blue polo, and gray pants.

"My name is Sean Wyatt. I am looking for a man by the name of Michel Steiner. I was told he runs this place." He decided to be direct and casual.

"I suppose you are here to ask about my father, no?" He kept writing furiously on the paper, never taking his eyes off it. "It is funny to me, Mr. Wyatt. No matter how much good a person does in the world, people still want to punish them for their sins. My father was a good man. He never believed in Hitler's war. And he never obeyed any order to kill anyone."

"I know, Herr Steiner." Sean used the German proper form. "I also understand that he built this business when he went AWOL from the army. Wanted to help people find jobs after the war and rebuild what the Nazis had torn down."

At this, the older man stopped his writing and looked up, peering over the top of his glasses. For a few seconds, he said nothing, just stared up at Sean, studying his face, trying to detect any hint of insincerity or deceit.

"You are not here to talk about Nazis?" he asked finally.

Sean motioned to the chair across from Steiner. The host nodded and leaned back, interested as to what his guest wanted.

"I'm not going to lie to you, Herr Steiner. I am researching something about the Nazis, but it's in regard to your books. I'm curious about the Riese Project."

Steiner tilted his head back and opened his mouth wide. "I see. And you're hoping you can figure out the mystery of whatever it was they were working on in the secret labs over at the mine."

Sean shook his head. "Only if it helps me get what I need."

The man raised his bushy, white eyebrows. "Oh? And what is that?"

Sean twisted his head around and looked outside, making sure no one was coming in. "Around thirty hours ago, a woman was taken from a research laboratory in Switzerland. She was abducted by a terrorist group. I'm not at liberty to give out more information than that. But if I don't figure out where they are and what they want in the next thirty-four hours, they're going to kill her. I can't let that happen."

The shock on the man's face could have stopped a train. "I wasn't aware of anything like that happening."

"You should watch the news a little more."

Steiner shook his head. "I don't like to watch such things. The world is so full of bad news now; it always makes me sad. I prefer to stay blissfully happy."

"I can understand that. But it doesn't change the fact that a young woman is going to be killed in cold blood if I don't figure out what she was working on and locate her in time." Sean stared through the man all the way to the back of the building.

Steiner could tell Sean was telling the truth, but there was still one thing he wanted to know. "What is this woman's name?"

Sean considered it for a second. It had already been blasted all over CNN and all the other news outlets. He wasn't exactly giving away classified information. "Franziska Ott."

For a few seconds, it looked as if Steiner was attempting to figure out whether or not he knew that name. He let out a sigh. "I'm sorry, but how does this young woman have anything to do with my father or die Glocke?"

Sean's face remained stone cold. "Her grandfather was one of the scientists working on the project."

Steiner drew in a long deep breath as his eyes widened. He contemplated the additional information and then stood up, walked over to the door, and flipped around the sign Sean assumed would let any visitors know that the office was closed. He twisted the long rod on the blinds, turning them down. The room was cast in shadow, and immediately became a much creepier place to be.

"I get so many people in here, poking fun at my theories with the Riese Project. They've seen my books and call me a crazy old man. But I've seen things, things that are not easily explained by the human mind or modern science." His voice carried a heavy sense of regret, and his face matched it. "My father did all he could to keep the Nazis from succeeding in their quest for the Wunderwaffe, the wonder weapon that would change the course of the war permanently, and make them completely unbeatable."

"Herr Steiner," Sean said, standing up. "Did you ever see die Glocke?" He took a shot in the dark.

"Me?" The man laughed a little at the notion. "No. I never saw it." Sean figured, but it was worth a try. "But I have seen many drawings of it. And my father was able to steal several calculations that were being used. He did it in an attempt to slow their progress."

Sean reached into his bag and pulled out the leather notebook. He showed it to the older man and laid it on his desk.

"Where did you get that?" Steiner asked, involuntarily walking back over to his workstation.

He eased back into his seat and picked up the book.

"It's a journal from Ott's grandfather. That notebook talks about all the math, theory, and the experiments that were done on the Riese Project."

Steiner carefully opened the book and turned the pages slowly. He didn't want to damage the pages of something so historically valuable. "Again I ask, where did you get this?" he said, never letting his eyes leave the book.

"It belonged to Dr. Ott. I found it in her apartment early yesterday afternoon."

The older man frowned. "In her apartment? Are you some kind of thief?"

"No, sir. I'm more of a specialist for hostage situations. Let's just say the United States government pays me to solve problems like this one." Sean's demeanor never changed. He wanted his host to understand that he was strong and would not bend until he had finished what he was sent to do.

"Ah. Like a detective," Steiner simplified it.

"Sort of. But with a much broader set of skills."

"I see." Steiner stopped turning the pages when he reached one of the last ones, one that contained the image of the bell-shaped object. "Mein Gott," he whispered. "Die Glocke."

Sean leaned forward in his seat and placed his hands on the desk's surface. "You've seen this drawing before?"

"Yes," the man nodded. He swallowed as he read each line of text. "I have seen this same image before, but I didn't know about all of this. This journal proves that the Nazis were trying to figure out a way to manipulate space-time and create their wonder weapon."

"Right. I get that," Sean said, leaning toward another point with the conversation. "But I need to know if there is anything else you might know that can help me find these people or maybe the bell itself." He stared at the man, unbending with his gaze. "An innocent woman's life depends on it."

The gravity of the situation wasn't lost on Steiner. Still, something was keeping him from being completely honest with Sean. When he spoke, it was with grave seriousness. "What I tell you now, you must never tell another person. It was a secret between my father and me. My mother might have known about it, but I doubt that. When it came to his time with the Nazis, my father was extremely secretive. He only told me about it because he felt like the information should be exposed someday. I put most of what I know in my books. They sold some copies and made a little extra money to keep this place going." He motioned to the aged office around them. "People do love a good mystery, especially when it comes to Nazis. But there were some details I left out. On purpose, of course."

"What details?" Sean tilted his body forward as if about to hear a huge secret.

"I'll let you see for yourself."

10

Miłków, Poland

Steiner stood up and motioned for Sean to follow. He led the way through a narrow, wood-paneled hallway to a smaller office in the back. A few stacks of paperwork sat atop a desk that was the twin of the one in the front. A few black-and-white pictures of a man and woman hung from the walls. Other than that, the room was sparsely decorated.

A picture of the man in the other images dangled from the wall directly behind the desk, the only thing that adorned the fake wood paneling in that section of the office. Steiner maneuvered behind the desk and grasped the picture frame on both sides. He lifted it carefully, unhooking the wire in the back from the nail on the wall and set the picture on the floor, leaning it against a gray filing cabinet. In the space where the picture had been was the front of a small black safe with a combination lock. It rested in a hole cut into the wall, a modification done either by the tenant or on request by the builder.

Sean raised an eyebrow, intrigued by what the older man could possibly be trying to hide.

His host spun the combination dial back and forth, doing it more slowly as he neared the final number. Sean averted his gaze to respect the man's privacy. The last thing he wanted to do was give the impression that he was some kind of thief. When Steiner finally stopped twisting the knob, the locking mechanism clicked, and he pulled down on the small metal latch. The safe door swung open, revealing a small stack of envelopes, a wad of cash wrapped in a rubber band, and a leather notebook that looked eerily similar to the one Sean had retrieved from Dr. Ott's apartment.

Steiner pushed the pile of money and envelopes to the back of the safe and retrieved the notebook. He turned around and sat at the desk, motioning Sean to take a seat in the lone chair on the other side. Sean did as requested, and pulled the chair close so he could see what the man was about to show him.

"My father left this to me when he died. He warned that there were things inside it that could be potentially dangerous, and that I should keep it safe."

Sean didn't think that keeping something so valuable in a cheaply made safe and in a fairly obvious hiding spot was exactly what the man's father meant, but he didn't want to offend his host.

Steiner went on. "I never really thought much about some of the details in this book. I used some of the information to entertain a few readers with wild conspiracy theories, but I didn't expect many people to believe them, even though I think there is a great deal of credibility to the things I gleaned from this journal.

"Father's original plan was to deliver this to the Allies, but in his fear of being persecuted for war crimes, he decided to lay low instead and keep the book hidden."

"Not a bad move on his part. The Allies went a little crazy when it came to hunting down old Nazis."

"Indeed." A twinge of regret filled his face. "No matter what amends they might have made." The moment passed, and Steiner got back to business. He turned the pages of the book to a page that featured a similar drawing to the one in Dr. Ott's book. He spun the journal around to give Sean a better view. He tapped the page. "See, almost the same image."

It was almost a photocopy match. There was no mistaking the bell's unique shape, its attachments, the doorframe on one side, and the way it was hovering in the air amid the circle of columns.

Steiner flipped a few more pages and pointed to the first paragraph of the handwritten notes. Unlike the book Sean had in his possession, this one lacked the high mathematical equations. "Can you read this?" he asked.

The script was written in German, which wasn't an issue, but the handwriting was fluid, almost like cursive, so it made understanding it a little more difficult. Still, Sean could manage.

He nodded and started reading through the passage. The translation to English happened automatically in his head.

Herr Ott told me that they are close to a breakthrough with the bell. If this happens, innocent people all over the world could be in grave danger. Herr Ott has done his best to sabotage progress, but now, it seems, they will achieve success. The only thing that seems to be on our side is time. The Allies push closer to the capital every day, which is why the high command has decided to relocate the bell, along with several of their officers, to somewhere in South America. According to the orders I saw, the voyage will be made on U-boat 1500. I was not aware that the German army had created that many submarines, but it appears some things have been kept secret from both the public, and those who would serve Hitler. The colonel in charge of the evacuation mission is Gilbert Shpurning. He is a hard man and pays close attention to detail. Any mission to try to steal the bell from their possession would be suicide. I was not chosen for escort detail.

I overheard another soldier say that we would be executing the scientists before the train leaves with the bell. While some of the researchers are just as evil as the Nazis themselves, Herr Ott has proven to be a good man and wants nothing to do with their plot. I am going to attempt to smuggle him out of the facility tonight. He can take safe harbor with family he has in Switzerland, should he be able to make the rest of the journey. It will be difficult for him, but all I can do is get him out of here alive.

I write all of this should anyone ever decide to expose the Nazis' evil schemes that took place here in Poland.

Unfortunately, should they learn about this journal, I would be executed. Because of that, I will take the secret of the bell's destination to my grave. Its dark science is not fit for this time, but perhaps someday, humanity will be ready for it.

Sean stopped reading and lifted his eyes. He turned the page but found nothing. "He said the name of the colonel in charge of the mission to transport the bell."

"Correct," Steiner said. The old man already knew the dots Sean was connecting. "He also mentioned a submarine called *U-1500*, but there is no record of that vessel anywhere in the archives. It did not exist, at least on paper."

"So you looked for it?"

Steiner sighed and glanced sideways down at the table for a split second, then returned his gaze to his guest. "I spent quite a bit of time searching for anything that had to do with the *U-1500*, years even. There was not a trace of it. Eventually, I came to the conclusion that the ship did not exist. If it did, the Nazis covered their tracks well. Obviously, they would not have gone to such trouble for something unimportant."

Sean thought about the passage for a minute and reexamined some of the sentences.

"It says that he took the bell's location to his grave." Sean peered up from the notebook. "I don't suppose your father let you know where that might be." Sean was hesitant to bring it up, but he had to know.

The host shook his head. "Sadly, no. Father believed that the world was not ready for that technology, and that if someone were to find the bell, its power could do immense damage. He died knowing where it was sent, but telling no one. If that submarine made it across the Atlantic Ocean, whoever was aboard it kept quiet, and the secret remains after all these years."

Another dead end, it seemed. "I don't suppose you know where Shpurning lived?"

"No. I wish I did. Though I don't know if that information would be helpful. The colonel may not have made the voyage. I searched for a few years, trying to find the name of the U-boat captain, but could discover nothing. The records on Shpurning are thin at best."

Sean took the conversation in a different direction. "I don't mean to be rude, and if I am overstepping my bounds, I apologize."

This made Steiner laugh. "Americans. So apologetic for everything. Go on, ask your question."

Sean blushed a little but went ahead. "Your father. Is the cemetery where he's buried close to here?"

Steiner didn't seem to be irritated by the query, but his face did change somewhat, to a more puzzled expression. "Yes, of course. Why do you ask?"

"It's just that..." Sean struggled to find a polite way to say it. "I'd like to take a look at his grave if that's okay with you. I won't disturb it or anything. I'm just curious to see if there's anything worth noting."

"I see. You think father may have left a clue at his burial site." Steiner leaned back in his chair and put his hands behind his head as he contemplated the notion. "Herr Wyatt, I have been to my father's grave hundreds of times since he died. I can tell you that I have never noticed anything peculiar, or anything that would make me think he left a clue to the whereabouts of the bell."

That tidbit was discouraging, but Sean wouldn't be brushed aside that easily. "Even so, if you don't mind, I would like to take a look for myself. I just want to make sure I leave no stone unturned. After all, a woman's life depends upon it."

Steiner contemplated the request for another twenty seconds. He shrugged as he spoke. "It's a public cemetery, Herr Wyatt. Anyone can go have a look."

"Will you take me there? I know you probably just opened the office, but it would be most helpful." Sean's eyes begged. He could probably find the cemetery with a set of simple directions, but then he would have to scour the graveyard in search of the one monument he needed.

Steiner laughed. "You can see we aren't very busy. We only get a few people in here every week. Ever since the mine closed and some of the other factories went out of business, there hasn't been much work in this village, unless you plan on working at one of the nearby farms." He stood up and removed a jacket from the back of the chair he'd been sitting in. "The cemetery isn't far from here. I can take a few minutes to show you."

Sean followed his host back out onto the sidewalk. The older man locked the door and dropped the keys into his pocket then started down the walkway. When they reached an intersection at the next block, the two crossed the street and continued in the same direction.

"The cemetery," Steiner pointed, "is right around that corner over there. It will come into view when we pass the stop sign." He apparently wanted to make small talk because he asked Sean how he'd come into the role he was working.

"It's a long story," he gave the cliché answer.

"Good ones usually are," Steiner quipped and flashed a clever grin.

Sean appreciated the wit. "I worked for the U.S. government for several years. I saw a lot of action in the field. More than I wanted. I needed a change, so I retired and went to work for my friend in the field of archaeology. My job was to secure priceless artifacts for transportation and get them to their destination safely."

"Oh?" Steiner raised his eyebrows and looked over at Sean. "That doesn't sound like a less stressful job to me."

"It wasn't. I found myself being shot at and chased, just like when I worked for the government. But there was a funny thing." He paused as they arrived at the next crosswalk, looked both ways, and then kept walking. "I spent so much time thinking about what my life would look like if I could just get away from those jobs and relax. You know?"

"Mmmhmm," Steiner said.

"I just wanted to run a shop on the beach and have a cabin in the woods. Maybe play some golf every now and then."

"You play golf?" The older man seemed a tad surprised.

"Not well," Sean admitted, half joking. His guide laughed, and he continued. "But no matter how much I tried to get away from that high-stress, dangerous lifestyle, it always seemed to find me."

Steiner stopped walking and seemed pensive for a moment before he turned and spoke. When he did, his tone was serious, but not stern, more matter-of-fact than anything. "We cannot run from our true selves, Herr Wyatt. Deep down inside, the person within us knows what it wants to be. It struggles to free itself of the lies we tell it. For some people, they tell themselves that they need to go to college and get a job in an office somewhere, when really what they want to do is start a business or travel, or become a missionary. No matter how much we lie to that person inside us, they will always find a way to get out. That, or they will make us miserable for our entire life until we set them free."

Steiner stared at Sean for a few seconds and then resumed walking. Sean thought about his words for a moment before catching up.

"I've never really heard it put that way, but I agree. I don't know if that little person inside of me really wants to do what I'm doing right now, but I do know that I feel like the world needs me to, and that's why I'm doing it."

The older man's face beamed. "The person inside knows that."

They reached the next corner, and Steiner pointed across the street. "There's the cemetery. My father's grave is in the middle. I'll show you where, and then I must return to the office."

There was something unsettled in Steiner's voice. The man pushed ahead, turning through the iron archway that rose up from stone pillars on either side. Sean couldn't read the Polish name of the cemetery that was displayed in wrought iron letters on the arch.

The graveyard was decorated with various trees: hemlocks, pines, and a few oaks here and there. Fresh flowers amid boxwoods and nandinas cast a sweet scent into the air. Sean always detested the smell of funerary flowers. It was one of the strongest smells his memory could recall. Normally, people would appreciate the wonderful scent of fresh flowers, but when it came to flowers in a cemetery or at a funeral home, they always nauseated Sean. He'd been to so many funerals growing up, the experiences made a permanent indent on his mind.

A tall stone wall wrapped around the entire cemetery, topped by wrought iron fencing with sharp points at the top of each rod. Some of the newer gravestones were in immaculate condition while the ones that dated beyond ninety years had fallen into ill repair. Some were barely legible. Others were crooked or falling over onto their sides. Occasionally, a mausoleum sprang up among the ordinary graves, an eternal tribute to someone who was willing and able to spend a little more in death than their less fortunate neighbors.

Sean followed Steiner through the winding maze of tall hedges, shaggy evergreen trees, and headstones. They arrived in the center of the graveyard, surrounded by dozens of stones that were marked from a similar era. Steiner stopped in front of one in particular. His face grew respectfully solemn as he stared at the name engraved on the stone.

"This is my father's grave," he said.

Max Steiner was born in 1916 and died in 1994. His wife, Lilia, was buried next to him, having died in 1985. Sean read the Biblical passage inscribed below the name and dates. It was one he recognized from the book of Psalms in the Old Testament reading, *I will fear no evil.*

A strange quote to include on one's headstone, but Sean figured it must have had personal meaning to the man, especially considering the older Steiner's close brushes with the Nazis. He'd likely seen a great deal of evil up close with his own eyes.

Over the name, Sean reread another line, one that both confused and surprised him. *May Saint Sebastian watch over you.*

Sean knelt down and passed over the line one more time. "What does this mean?" he asked. Steiner was still standing behind him with a regret-filled face.

"Which part?" Sean answered by pointing at the top sentence on the stone. "Oh. Saint Sebastian?" Sean nodded. "I am not entirely sure. Father rarely spoke of a patron saint. I would assume that was the one he chose, though I do not know why. He was never a deeply religious man. That fact always made me question why that sentence was on his headstone. It was what he wanted, though."

Sean thought for a second. "This isn't the first place I've seen that. It's in Ott's journal as well. The exact same line."

It could mean only one thing. The two were connected somehow and held a deeper meaning than Sean or anyone else had first suspected. The only question was what *was* that connection?

He pulled out his phone and sent a quick text message to Tommy, asking him to dig up all he could about Saint Sebastian. Sean leaned closer to the stone, staring hard at a small emblem etched into the surface. His eyes widened. Carved into the smooth stone was the shape of a bell, no longer than two inches and maybe an inch wide. Four numbers surrounded it. On the left side, a one. On top was a five. The right side of the bell and the bottom both had zeroes.

It's 1500. The same number as the U-boat that was rumored to carry the strange object.

Sean's heart began to beat. *How are the two connected? Why is Saint Sebastian mentioned twice? What does it have to do with the U-boat? And where did it end up?*

The thoughts stormed through his mind, and he couldn't sort them all out at once. He stood up and turned around to face Steiner. "This has been very helpful," he said. "I hope I haven't taken up too much of your time."

"Not at all," Steiner smiled and shook his head. "If anyone can put an ending to this mystery, I would be most grateful. My father went to his grave with a very serious and deep secret. I believe that had he wanted to keep it completely hidden, he would not have left little clues lying around."

"I agree," Sean offered. His eyes narrowed at the sight of movement a hundred feet away, just beyond a row of headstones.

Sean instinctively grabbed his weapon and held it low, not wanting to alarm Steiner too much. The sudden movement took the older man aback. The weapon was also disconcerting. "What are you doing?" he asked, bewildered.

"Herr Steiner, stay here, and keep low. I believe we were followed."

Sean turned and ducked behind a wide headstone. Someone knew he was here, but how was that even possible? He peeked over the top and motioned for Steiner to join him. Steiner's immediate concern was reaffirmed when he glanced back the way they'd come and saw two men moving quickly, keeping low behind the head-stones and other monuments as they approached.

He ducked for cover where Sean had holed up and waited for orders. "Who are those men? What should we do?"

"Not sure who they are," Sean said. "First I've seen them, although they could be the guys I ran into in Switzerland." It was impossible to know since the approaching threat was clad in scarves that covered half of their faces and wore black baseball caps on their heads. In the quiet solitude of the empty, small town cemetery, no one would see them and raise an alarm. Sean noted the silencers on the ends of the weapons the men carried.

He gripped his own weapon and snapped on a three-inch long, black metal box to his barrel. The suppressor was unlike any he'd seen on the market, a product from his friend at DARPA. This new kind of silencer was nearly half the length of standard ones, and didn't have to screw into place. Grooved clasps locked it onto the end of a weapon like a vice grip. In field tests, the prototypes had endured several hundred pounds of pressure before the metal succumbed and snapped free. On the up side, even when it did, the guns weren't damaged other than a few scratches, so the shooter could continue using the weapon, albeit in a much louder capacity.

Sean kept his back to the gravestone and looked toward the back of the cemetery. At the moment, the men were only approaching from the front, which meant they could go out the back door, if there was one.

"Is there a way out the other end of the cemetery?" Sean asked quietly.

Steiner followed his gaze toward a thick stand of willows, oak, and pine. The walls on either side extended over a small rise and beyond. The older man nodded. "Yes, there is a gate."

A little luck after all.

"But it is usually locked."

Of course it is.

Sean thought for a second and took a peek back around the side of the headstone. A splinter of concern shot through his spine. The men were gone. Either they had passed by, gone around a different direction, or..."

The stone next to his face exploded, sending fragments of gray shrapnel past his face. One of the broken pieces struck his cheek just below the eye, and he pulled back instantly. The spot on his face throbbed. Sean glanced back over at Steiner who stared at him with mouth agape.

"Is it bleeding?" Sean asked, trying to sound as casual as possible.

Steiner gave a terrified nod.

Sean pursed his lips for a second. He pulled his body back to where he'd been and quickly surveyed their right flank. Whoever the guy was that took the shot had gone back to his hiding place. An old feeling crept into Sean's mind, and he turned around just in time to see another attacker pop out from behind a pine tree on the left flank.

Sean fired four rapid shots, but range and accuracy was an issue with the compact weapon, no matter how good he was with it. Two of the bullets burrowed into the tree, the other two ended as plumes of dirt and grass near his target's boots.

Even though he didn't hit the man, the shots did enough to scare him back to cover. Three more muffled shots came from the center of the makeshift battlefield. Sean ducked back down as the rounds cracked into the hard front of the gravestone.

"We're going to have to make a run for it," Sean said. He leaned forward and fired two shots to the right, then two to the left. Both men had started to peek around the trees they were using for cover. Sean's volley sent them back. He poked the gun over the top of the headstone and fired two more. On the third trigger pull, the gun merely clicked.

"We'll be easy targets if we do that," Steiner protested.

Sean pushed the button on the side of his gun's grip and watched the empty magazine slide out and fall to the grass. In an instant, he'd retrieved a full one from the carrier attached to his holster strap and smacked it into place. He pulled back the slide and stared hard at the old man.

"When I start shooting, you go as fast as you can. Get over the hill and out the back. I'll be right behind you."

Steiner frowned. "How many of those bullets do you have?"

"Don't worry about that, Herr Steiner. Just go. Stay low, and use the headstones for cover."

The older man seemed reluctant, but there was no time to argue.

"Ready?" Sean asked. The question was rhetorical. He crouched behind the headstone and fired a shot straight at the man forty feet away who was poking his head around the edge and trying to line up a shot. Sean's round pinged off the other gravestone in a small dust cloud, but it did the job, sending the attacker reeling for cover once more.

He turned left again, ready to fire, but the man on that side was still behind cover. A bullet ripped through the edge of Sean's shoulder from the backside. The searing hot pain instantly called his attention to the right flank. The man who'd shot tucked back against the tree, but this time left the front of a black boot exposed. Sean lined up the foot carefully and squeezed the trigger.

The foot popped in an eruption of red and black, causing the man to bend forward involuntarily to grab at the destroyed appendage. The move was a fatal mistake, and Sean sent two more rounds at him, the first missing narrowly behind the target, the second going through the man's neck.

Sean didn't wait to see the man collapse to the ground. He'd already returned his attention to the left flank and the man in the center. Out of the corner of his eye, he could see Steiner working his way back through the headstones, attempting to stay as low as he could. Sean squeezed off another shot at the man to the left and started slinking backward, ducking behind a headstone each time he reached one. With the guy still on the left, the farther back in the cemetery they went, the clearer the shot from that flank would be. Sean knew he needed to put himself between the shooter and Steiner if the older man was to have a chance of escaping.

He shifted to the left and fired another shot down the center column. The attacker in the middle ducked out of the way but reappeared and fired several shots of his own. The bullets bounced off the stones around Sean, but he realized the men were pressing now. The one on the left moved up the side, taking three shots to cover himself before he sprinted to the next tree. Sean watched as the man repeated the process a second time, trying to cut off the angle Sean was hurrying to protect.

Sean saw the gun stick out from behind an ancient oak, pointing in Steiner's direction. From the deliberateness of the movement, Sean knew he was lining up the weapon to take the perfect shot at the old man.

Sean crouched on one knee and wielded his weapon, snapping off three more shots, each one missing the target and sinking into the trunk's thick wood. He saw the barrel fire four times, puffing a thin waft of smoke and flame from the tip. Sean glanced back and saw Steiner drop to the ground behind a tall, narrow headstone. Clenching his teeth, Sean rose from his cover and sent three shots at the man in the center, who had stood up and was charging toward him. The volley sent him diving out of the way, one of the rounds barely missing his legs, instead striking the dirt just beyond. Sean sprinted toward the oak and caught the man just as he'd stepped out to fire into the middle.

The attacker's eyes went wide with surprise for a moment, not realizing Sean had abandoned the safety of the headstones. The American launched into the air, leading with the barrel of his gun, and squeezed the trigger repeatedly until it clicked again.

Three hollow points found their mark squarely in the man's chest. He fell backward, firing one harmless shot into the air before hitting a cluster of tangled tree roots on the ground. The body shivered for a few seconds and then went limp.

More bullets screamed through the air at Sean's position, and he pressed up against the tree for a second to shield himself from the onslaught. Unconsciously, he hit the release button on his gun. The empty magazine dropped to the ground and he mechanically inserted the last full clip he had. He looked down at the body and had an idea. The man was strong, but thin, probably about the same height and weight as Sean.

He stepped over to the dead man, careful to keep out of the last attacker's line of sight, and grabbed the body by the back of the collar. He jerked it up, and quickly removed the man's jacket, then dropped the body to the ground and returned to the tree. Sean swallowed hard and took a deep breath. He gave another look back to where Steiner had fallen, but from what he could tell, the man wasn't moving. He took another breath and poked the jacket out from the right side of the tree trunk.

The other attacker's weapon popped several times, ripping through the right half of the coat. Sean kept his grip on the collar of the decoy, making it appear as though whoever was there was still standing against the tree. Then he wrapped his right arm around the tree and lined up the man in the center. He pulled the trigger, and the target on the other end of his sight shuddered for a second before falling prostrate to the ground.

Sean dropped the jacket and hurried back into the rows of graves. He kept his weapon at the ready, checking various trees and monuments he thought could be threatening positions of attack as he made his way over to where Steiner had fallen.

He reached the older man and immediately saw Steiner was bleeding through his sweater vest. Two bullets had found their mark in his side. Even though Sean knew they were mortal wounds, he tried to encourage the man.

Sean cradled the man's head as he spoke, staring into nearly vacant eyes. "Stay with me, Herr Steiner. Everything's going to be okay. I'm calling an ambulance right now."

Steiner coughed and smiled through a grimace. He shook his head. "An ambulance won't help me now, young man. We both know that. Just leave me be."

"I can't do that," Sean said with determination. "I don't leave friends behind."

"I..." Steiner winced again. "I appreciate the sentiment, Sean. But I have a feeling I'm going to have the answers you seek before you do." The insinuation wasn't lost on Sean, and he swallowed back the pain.

Inside, he cursed himself for bringing the older man into the fray. He'd put Steiner in harm's way and been unable to protect him.

Steiner could see the conflict and pain in Sean's eyes. "Do not blame yourself," he said in a whisper. "I've lived a good life. I am ready."

He smiled again even though he was in tremendous agony.

"I'll see my father soon. It is okay, Sean. I am at peace. Continue your quest." He gasped for another breath. The words were more difficult now. "Protect the innocent. This...die Glocke must not...fall...into the wrong...hands." Steiner's lips quivered, and the last breath of air escaped from his lungs. His eyes went still, staring at the sky. The head became heavier in Sean's hands as it went limp.

A tear welled in Sean's right eye, but he fought it back and clenched his teeth. He laid Steiner's head down on the ground gently, crossed the man's hands over his chest, and pulled the eyelids closed.

Moments like this were harder than any others in the line of duty. Sean knew he had to move fast. If there were three men on his heels, there would likely be more. He needed to find out who was after him. On top of that, he had to find where that U-boat went. There was nothing he could do to help Steiner now. And despite the fact that his death was tragic, Sean knew he had to focus on the living.

There would be plenty of time for honoring the dead later. Ignoring the insensitive nature of what he was doing, Sean reached into the man's front pocket and removed the set of keys he'd seen Steiner put there when they left the office less than a half hour ago.

He put his weapon back in its holster and pulled out his phone. A few seconds later, Emily answered as Sean walked over to the dead man by the tree.

"What's your status, Zero?" she asked stoically.

"Three assets terminated. Not sure how they found me, but they did. One civilian casualty. There was nothing I could do. We were ambushed." He tried to speak without much regret, but it swelled up inside him anyway. Steiner was a good man, and the guilt for having involved him was something Sean would have to deal with sooner or later. At the moment, it would need to be later.

There was silence on the other end for a few seconds. "Are you still on the scene?"

"Affirmative," Sean answered. "I'm getting out now. Just checking one thing before I go."

He knelt down and pressed the phone against his ear as he searched the pockets of the dead man. He found a Lithuanian passport, a wad of Euros, and a set of keys. He took a picture of the passport name and picture, then dropped it onto the dead man's chest.

"I'm going to send you a picture. It's the passport I found on one of the assets. Find out who he is and who he works for."

"Probably an alias, but I'll run it," she answered. "You need an extract?"

"Not yet," he said, picking up his pace and running over to the other dead assailant lying on his face in the middle of the cemetery.

He reached the other body and sifted through the various pockets until he found what he was looking for. Similarly, the man had a wad of cash and a foreign passport. This one was from the Republic of Georgia. "Looks like they're using identification from former Soviet states," he said, informing Emily of what he'd found. "I'm sending you another image to run."

He repeated the process he'd used with the previous passport and hit send.

"Any leads with what we're looking for?"

Sean started jogging, weaving between the headstones and back onto the narrow concrete path leading to the graveyard entrance. "Not sure yet. Hopefully, I'll know something soon. For the time being, I need to get back across the border into Germany. I'll let you know what I find out later."

"Okay," she said, though her voice indicated that the information was anything but. "We're running out of time."

11

Miłków, Poland

When Sean reached the sidewalk along the street, he slowed his pace to a brisk walk. The last thing he wanted to do was be the memorable face of the man that walked away from a quadruple homicide in a cemetery in a quiet Polish town. Fortunately, the gunplay hadn't been noticed. There was so little vehicular and pedestrian traffic that no one heard the suppressed weapons being fired. An older woman with thick, gray hair and a puffy sky-blue shirt hobbled down the sidewalk a few blocks up but never gave any indication she was aware of what had just occurred. Bad news was that his shoulder was bleeding. The stinging pain surged through his arm and up his neck, telling him he needed to check the wound as soon as possible. He needed to get to the bag he'd left in Steiner's office. Sean always kept a small emergency first aid kit tucked away inside his rucksack. It wasn't much, but it could keep the wound from getting infected and from the feel of it, he'd only require a few stitches at most.

His thoughts returned to the shootout in the cemetery. Emily would notify the authorities about the incident via an anonymous tip, thus preventing an innocent visitor to the graveyard from discovering dead bodies lying around above ground. The visual ran through Sean's head for an instant, and he pictured the hysteria that would ensue.

He'd text Emily when he crossed back into Germany so she'd know he made it out.

Sean traced his steps back to Steiner's office, the entire time attempting to conceal his wound without looking like he was trying to hide something. When he reached the office he continued walking, passing the front door and windows. He stopped at the next intersection and made a hard left, around to the back of the strip of main street businesses. Once he was behind the buildings, he found the door he was looking for corresponding with Steiner's office and fished the keys out of his pocket. He'd not seen which key the older man had used to lock up, but lucky for Sean, there were only three to choose from, and one was clearly a car key.

He got it right on the first guess, and the lock turned easily, opening the door into the rear of the office.

Sean hurried through an empty room that appeared to have once housed file storage and then into the short corridor leading to the front of the building. He turned right into the side office and stepped around behind the desk. He grabbed his rucksack off the desk and stuck his hand inside it, feeling around for the blue vinyl pouch. His fingers found what he was looking for and set it on the desk. Next, he stripped down to his bare chest and set his clothes on the back of the chair. He examined the wound and was glad to see it was as he'd suspected. The bullet had taken out a chunk of his shoulder, but it missed bone and muscle.

He opened up the kit and set to sterilizing the wound with a peroxide swab. The chemicals sent a new sting through the tear in his skin as it foamed around the congealing blood. Satisfied it was sterile enough, Sean took a piece of adhesive gauze from the pack and pressed it hard against the wound. Once he'd smoothed out the tape he zipped up the emergency kit and stuck it back in the bag.

He put his shirt back on and noticed the leather-bound journals sitting nearby. It wasn't irreverent to take them. At least that's what he told himself. He needed the books. With a sigh, Sean stuffed both leather-bound journals into his rucksack, slung the strap over his shoulder and strode quickly back into the hallway. A rapid check in the front office, the hall, and the storage room told him there were no surveillance cameras, a fact that didn't surprise him. Other than the safe in his little office, there was nothing of value in the place.

He strode back to the rear of the building and locked the door. Another look around to make sure no one noticed him, and Sean took off at an Olympic-paced walk. Passing a dumpster, he lifted the lid and dropped the keys inside. No need to have that extra piece of evidence on him.

Four minutes later, he was back in his car and steering it out onto the main road. He glanced in the rearview mirror and watched the sleepy village fade into the forests and hills on the horizon. His eyes kept looking in that direction every thirty seconds for the next hour. Paranoia was a good friend to have in situations where danger could creep up from behind at any moment. It forced Sean to stay focused, sharp.

Crossing the border into Germany proved to be easy enough. A quick stop with the passport control officer, and he was back on the road without much fuss. The dark-haired border patrol officer barely even glanced over Sean's identification. Over the years, going from one country to another had almost become as easy as travel between states back in the U.S. The stops on the borders were more like toll-booths than anything else.

Once he was through and back in Germany, Sean kept driving. He wasn't exactly sure where to go, so he steered the vehicle in the direction of Frankfurt, figuring if he had to fly somewhere, that would be the best place to take off.

He merged with a pack of other cars onto the Autobahn leading south and started to turn on the radio before he felt his phone vibrating against his leg. A moment of dread sprang up in his gut, but he forced it away, a task made much easier when he looked at the caller ID on the screen.

It was Tommy.

"Hey, man," he said coolly in an attempt not to sound even the slightest bit nerve-wracked.

"We were able to dig up that information you requested, though we're not sure it's going to be as helpful as you'd like." Tommy waited for a response before he continued.

"Some info is better than none." Sean switched lanes to let a red Mercedes Benz speed by.

Tommy took an audible breath on the other end. "I agree. So here it is. Saint Sebastian was a third-century Christian who was martyred in AD 288."

"Oh. During Diocletian's persecution of the Christians."

"Right," Tommy confirmed. "Most images suggest he was killed with arrows, but there are some legends that say he spoke out against the emperor and was clubbed to death. No one's really got anything definitive on that."

Sean interrupted again. "Any idea how that bit of information would be pertinent today?"

"Not sure. I suppose it would depend on the context."

Sean thought for a second before answering. "He doesn't happen to have anything to do with the world ending or any sort of post-apocalyptic prophecy, does he?"

"I don't think so. He was just a man who died for his faith. A commoner. However, there is another possibility that ties into a mysterious happening during World War II."

"I'm all ears." Sean switched lanes to get around an eighteen-wheeler and then swerved back.

"Remember before when you asked me to search for information about German U-boats going to South America? Well, we were able to dig up some interesting stuff. Tara and Alex searched the old naval archives and cross-referenced everything with dates close to the end of the war, as well as possible destinations. There is a city on the southern tip of Argentina called *San Sebastián*. It's a decent-sized coastal town with a huge bay that forms a sort of natural harbor. The pictures actually look pretty amazing."

"Focus," Sean sensed his friend getting off track.

"Right. So anyway, San Sebastián could explain why you've seen that name a few times in its European form, *Saint Sebastian*."

He let Sean absorb the news.

"Outstanding," Sean said emphatically.

"Well, let's not count our chickens just yet. However, there is another piece to the puzzle that adds a little more credence to the San Sebastián theory." Sean waited while his friend pulled up some additional info, probably in another document or web page on his computer. "In the naval archives I mentioned earlier, Tara and Alex discovered a peculiar incident. A captain by the name of Jack Harris aboard the *USS Slater* logged a short report about a potential U-boat sighting in one of the lanes between Africa and South America. The event was recorded on May 3, 1945, just a few days before Hitler and his wife ended their lives in the Führer's bunker. Harris was very detailed about the event in his log, and there are some eerie comments made about the whole thing."

"Eerie?"

"Yeah. It seems just before the sub appeared, all of the Slater's instrumentation failed. I'm talking electronics, radar, everything. Harris also claimed that the weather was clear, but when the sub disappeared, a strange fog had drifted into the area, and when it dissipated, the U-boat was gone."

Sean listened closely. "That certainly is an odd sequence of events."

"Sure is. Harris said they started firing on the sub, but it vanished before they could take it down."

"Went below the surface?"

"No," Tommy corrected. "Like it completely disappeared into thin air. And just before it did, the ship's crew reported the same instrument malfunction from before the U-boat showed up."

Tommy was right. It was beyond weird. Sean had heard of different reports of this nature from the archives. Usually, they had to do with UFO sightings, most of the time revolving around the Nevada or New Mexico deserts. There were a few other odd reports, such as the stories and legends surrounding the Bermuda Triangle, but this didn't have anything to do with any of those things. According to what Tommy said, this event occurred far outside of the Bermuda Triangle, and it wasn't aliens they were seeing but a German submarine, far outside its normal route of operation.

He looked out the window as he pondered the details he'd been given. A VW minivan passed by, loaded down with three kids in the back and two worn-out-looking parents in the front. The child at the window closest to Sean was staring at him with his mouth opened wide and lips pressed to the glass. *I feel the same way, kid,* Sean thought.

"You still there?" Tommy asked, plucking Sean from his thoughts.

"Yeah. I'm here. Just trying to process all this."

"It's a mind job, that's for sure. I don't know if it helps with what you're looking for. It just struck me as one of the few things in the archives that really stuck out."

"Actually, this might be exactly what we needed. If a U-boat was able to appear and disappear right in front of an entire ship full of sailors at the same time their instruments went down, I'd say that's the sub I'm looking for."

A silent moment descended on their conversation before Tommy spoke up again. "You're still not going to tell me what it is you're trying to figure out, are you?"

Sean laughed. "Can't do that, buddy. Working for old friends. That's all I can say."

"I understand. But if you're looking for a German U-boat that can do what those reports said, it sounds like you're into something heavy, like dealing with wormhole technology or something."

"I'll let you bend your mind around theories, buddy. All I know is, I've got to get to Argentina as fast as possible."

"Well, before you go, we went ahead and did a search of German names in the region of San Sebastián. We found a few that were of interest. You should probably check those out first if that's where you're headed."

Sean chuckled. Tommy and his assistants were able to dig up nearly any kind of information. While the rest of the world could find what they needed through their favorite search engines, Sean was certain Tommy and the other two had other resources at their disposal.

"How'd you do that?"

"Don't worry about it. You have your secrets. I have mine."

"Fair enough."

"The first person you're looking for is a guy by the name of Alfred Wolfz. I'll send you his address. He's in his sixties. Definitely has German roots. There's not much on his father, which makes me think he was one of the Nazis who escaped the country. The other one is a woman, also in her sixties, named Irena Stoepel. Same kind of background. Definitely German heritage. And just like with Wolfz, it's pretty sketchy."

"What have you got on their families?" Sean pressed his luck. The more he could find out now, the better chance he would have of getting a response from either person when he arrived in Argentina.

"Nothing really. Wolfz had a wife, she's deceased. Kids moved away, not sure where. He lives alone now. Stoepel never married. She also lives by herself in a villa overlooking the coast."

"Sounds like she's doing well for herself. Wonder if there was some kind of trust fund that got her started in life." He let the rest of his idea speak for itself.

"Could be. Anyway, I hope this helps. I'm giving a keynote here in Atlanta in a few hours, so I've got to get going."

"It helps a lot. Thanks, Tommy."

"No problem. Always happy to help."

Sean ended the call and focused on the road. His foot pressed on the accelerator, easing the car into a higher rate of speed. A quick check of the clock on the dashboard told him it was still late in the morning. He picked his phone up and found the contact he needed then hit the green button.

"That was fast." Emily answered on the other end. Always direct.

"Running out of time," Sean said. "But I'm making progress. Would be nice if the terrorists would give us another day."

"Yeah, not gonna happen."

"I figured. I'm en route back to Frankfurt. I need a ride to Argentina."

She listened to his request. "Argentina, huh? You going to look for old Nazis down there?"

"Something like that."

"I sure hope you're not chasing a wild goose on this one. If you fly down there, and it turns out to be nothing..."

He cut her off, "I know. Dr. Ott will be dead. It's the only lead we've got. And it's the only one that makes sense. Besides, we're down to the last quarter here. Have to gamble and throw a hail Mary."

"A football *and* a poker reference in the same sentence? Impressive."

He blew off the snide comment. "Just have the plane ready to roll when I get there."

"Which will be?"

"In a few hours. I just got into Germany a few minutes ago."

She sighed. "All right. I'll have a private plane ready and waiting when you get there."

"You coming with me?"

"No," she laughed. "I have business to attend to here in Europe. But I'll be monitoring your whereabouts."

"Comforting." It was his turn to be snarky.

"It should be," she returned.

"I'll be in touch when I'm on Argentinean time."

He hit end and set the phone back down on the leather passenger seat.

Ahead, the sky was crystal clear, and the sun shone brightly down on the rolling north German foothills. Other less-seasoned veterans of the trade would probably take the good weather as a positive sign. Sean wasn't naive, though. He knew that the journey was far from over, and before it ended, there would be heavy storms again.

12

"We're going to need to make a move, sir. We can't wait any longer."

Admiral McClain pondered the comment. He held his phone against his ear as he walked through the hallway leading into his bedroom. The lavish master bedroom featured high recessed ceilings, bronze-colored curtains, and a few abstract paintings his decorator had picked out.

A chestnut-brown suitcase was laid out on his bed, the edge of it flush with the walnut footboard. He'd finished packing before his man had called. It was just a matter of getting a few more essentials before he was ready to leave. He tossed a toothbrush enclosed in a Ziploc bag into the suitcase and closed it shut.

"I agree. Time is running out on this whole thing." He walked over to a bedroom door that led onto a small balcony. Beyond the doorway windows was a small white bistro table with two matching wooden chairs. He stared out at the early morning sunrise coming up over the city. "I heard some people were killed in Poland."

A few silent seconds passed before the man on the other end of the line responded. "I heard the same."

"The Axis asset made it out alive, though." It was almost a question.

"He did."

McClain had already heard about the incident at the cemetery. Concern washed over him. "That particular asset could be trouble. He tends to make a mess of things wherever he goes. The last thing we need is him getting in the way."

"I'll handle it, sir."

"See to it that you do. This is not a game we're playing. I knew that Emily Starks interfering with operations would be a problem. Proceed as necessary. I'm getting on a plane in two hours. I sent you the rendezvous point a few minutes ago. Make sure you and your team are on a jet and en route within the hour."

"Yes, sir."

McClain ended the call. He slid the device into his pocket and ran both hands through his hair. Managing operations like this one had been something he'd done for the last few decades. Usually, he was more hands off than right now. But there were things that had to be overseen that could not be trusted to underlings. Sometimes, the people who did the ground work, the foot soldiers, had to be micromanaged. In some ways, they actually wanted that. If they were left to their own thoughts or devices, things could get out of hand quickly.

The stakes were way too high to allow that to happen.

The admiral grabbed a windbreaker and set it next to his suitcase. It was warm in D.C., but he always got a chill when traveling on a plane, even on the private government planes like the one he'd be boarding soon. He grabbed the zipper on the suitcase and pulled it around the edge, carefully stuffing a loose piece of fabric from a heavy coat back into the case.

He grabbed the bag and his laptop case and headed down the stairs to the carriage park where he kept his car. Three minutes later, he was out on the road and heading west, away from the city. Since his flight was in the early morning hours, driving into town to Reagan would have been a huge mistake. Arlington County would be bogged down, and the beltway would be a parking lot for hours. Even though it was more than twenty miles outside of town, getting to Dulles would be faster since he'd be going against the traffic.

As he expected, the drive took barely over half an hour. McClain went through one of the private airline security checkpoints, happily showing off the badge that told the man at the booth just who he was dealing with. The young man gave a short salute, which the admiral returned before accelerating through the open gate.

He drove around to one of the outlying hangars and parked outside one that was unmarked. An American flag flapped vigorously in the wind next to it. A white G6 jet's nose poked out through the massive doorway. There were no couriers to help him with his bags. To be honest, he didn't want to be waited on like that. Not yet anyway. There would be a time for that soon enough when he retired. For now, he was still just another relic from a forgotten time.

The admiral walked around the corner of the hangar and found a few workers milling around. A pretty young woman stood at the top of the steps leading into the airplane's cabin. The engines hadn't been revved up yet, and wouldn't be until the plane had been pulled out of its parking space. McClain handed off the suitcase to one of the men in an orange vest and made his way over to the steps.

At the top, the blonde with the low-cut button-up short-sleeved shirt smiled, showing teeth as bright as snow. "Welcome aboard, Admiral. I hope your drive wasn't too bad with the morning traffic."

She obviously didn't think about the direction he'd come. "Not too bad at all, Miss...?"

"Elkins," she answered.

"Not too bad, Miss Elkins."

"Excellent, sir. If you'll make your way back to the main cabin, we will begin preparations for takeoff. Once we're in the air, breakfast will be served."

"Terrific," he said, brandishing a fake smile. Breakfast did sound good, but eating was the last thing on his mind.

He headed where the young woman had motioned with her hand and found his way into a luxuriously appointed area. Beige leather seemed to be everywhere. It bound the chairs and molding along the edges just above the windows. Cherry wood accents contrasted the pale tones of the leather.

McClain found his way over to one of the empty seats and sank down into it. He laid his laptop case on the floor next to his feet, and leaned the chair back. Other than the flight attendant and the pilots, he was the only one on board. It was a surreal feeling after all those years of flying coach, occasionally getting to step up to first class. *This is the way people were meant to fly,* he thought.

Miss Elkins entered through the open doorway, still smiling as broadly as she had before. "Could I get you a cup of coffee while we're waiting to take off?"

"That would be lovely," the admiral answered, giving his best grin. "Thank you."

She acknowledged his comment with an elongated nod, and then went to the back to fetch the coffee pot. At this point, McClain didn't even care if the coffee was good or not. It could have been brewed yesterday. This was the life.

Soon, he knew that doing things this extravagantly would be the norm not the exception. He just had to make sure everything went according to plan.

The flight attendant returned with a steaming cup of hot coffee on a silver platter. *Literally, a silver platter,* McClain thought. He accepted the cup, as graciously as possible, and picked up one of the sugar packets lying next to a tiny carafe of cream.

She lingered nearby for a moment to make sure everything was to his liking. "We should be in Buenos Aires around 9:00 pm tonight. In Argentinean time, it will be 11:00 pm."

A brutally long flight. But necessary. No way he would ever try to fly that far in economy class. Not anymore. But doing it this way? No problem.

He sat back and took a long sip of his coffee.

It wasn't bad after all.

13

San Sebastián, Argentina

Sean's flight seemed to last all night. By the time he arrived in Buenos Aires, it was well past one in the morning. Fortunately, the flight had been a comfortable one. The seats aboard the private airplane folded down into beds, which allowed him to get some light sleep along the way. Sean rarely experienced a solid eight hours of sleep. Naps, however, were something he could do effectively. During the long flight, he got at least four to five hours of sleep, when it was all added together.

After another three hours of sleeping in the hotel, he was taken back to the airport and flown to the southern town of San Sebastián by seaplane.

During all of his adventures and missions, Sean had never actually been on a seaplane before. He'd started to think that they only existed in movies and television shows. The pilot was a gruff man in his late fifties. He had a scruffy beard with thick patches of gray mingled in streaks of brown, and went by the name of Kurt Dothan. A tattoo on his right forearm told Sean all he needed to know about his pilot's toughness. It was a skull with a lightning bolt through it, sitting atop a black shield. The words *Airborne Rangers* wrapped around the image.

There was a small airport outside San Sebastián, but getting a flight there unnoticed had been tricky. With a smaller aircraft, they could fly in and out without too many prying eyes bearing witness. Not to mention flights in and out were rare. Flying in with the government jet would get a lot of attention.

Sean was starting to rethink that logic as the noisy, dilapidated contraption muscled its way through the lower reaches of the atmosphere, nearing the coved city.

"The landings can sometimes be a little rough," the pilot informed him. The only thing missing from the guy's smuggler-like appearance was a cigar and a sidearm. Sean figured the man's weapon was probably in a glove box somewhere within reach. "All depends on how the sea is acting that day."

"Good to know." It was rare when Sean sat in a plane cockpit. He didn't mind it, though it lacked the lavish luxuries of the private jet.

Out the window, the majestic hills rolled into low mountains. Snow covered two thirds of them. Sean could see skiers and snowboarders coasting down the slopes of a nearby resort. From such a distance, the people looked like tiny, pleasure-seeking ants. He'd always wanted to come to Argentina for some "summer snowboarding" but the chance hadn't presented itself yet. He was glad he'd brought a jacket on the trip, but going deep into South America in the heart of their winter would mean he'd need to visit a local store and buy a heavier coat.

Reading his mind, the pilot informed Sean that the local temperature in San Sebastián Bay was a balmy thirty-seven degrees Fahrenheit.

The pilot looped the plane over the bay and back out beyond the coast, sizing up where the water would be calmest. The beaches were completely vacant, an odd sight for such a picturesque place. Sean imagined that in the summer, thousands of people would cover the white beaches, soaking up every ounce of warm sunshine they could. The bay, too, was absent of any activity, save a lone fishing boat that seemed either anchored in the middle of the cove or happy to stay within the confines of the surrounding hillsides.

"How'd you come to live in Argentina?" Sean asked out of sheer curiosity.

Dothan sniffled and wiped his nose with the back of his hand. "I grew up in Alaska. Been flying these kinds of planes since I was a boy. I used to work for the government."

Sean's eyebrows rose slightly, but he let the man continue talking. The pilot laughed. "Nothing cool like a spy or anything like that. I did deliveries for different government branches in Alaska."

"That's a long way from here," Sean said, staring out over the setting.

"That was the idea," Dothan said.

"You live in Buenos Aires?"

The pilot nodded. "Yep. I usually make one or two of these runs a week. Takes care of the bills and keeps me in the air, which is where I prefer to be."

"Any particular reason you chose Argentina?"

Dothan glanced over at Sean as he leveled out the plane and began the final descent. It was the kind of look that wondered why he asked. "Have you seen the women down here? Absolutely stunning."

An awkward moment passed before Dothan broke out into laughter. Sean smiled, and allowed himself to chuckle at the comment. "Point taken."

The plane's floats skidded over the top of the dark-blue water, cutting through the choppy surface with relative ease. As the aircraft started to settle deeper into the sea it began to bounce around.

"Water's a little rough today. Nothing out of the ordinary," Dothan informed his passenger.

Sean gripped a handle on the side of the cockpit but trusted what the pilot said. Their speed slowed rapidly, and Dothan cut the engines down to a high idle, steering the plane to an outlying dock off the outer coast of the bay. At the land end of the wooden structure, a small red building had been constructed. Sean wasn't sure what its purpose might be, but it appeared to be unoccupied at the moment.

"I'm going to let you out over there," the pilot said. "You'll need to huff it into town from here. Shouldn't take you more than twenty minutes."

For a second, Sean longed for the comforts of a car that could drive him around, but he didn't complain. He'd been in worse conditions. Although now getting that heavier coat would definitely be his first priority.

"You just gonna hang out here?" Sean asked.

"I'll be in that red building if you need me." He pointed at the structure Sean had noticed earlier.

"That's yours?"

Dothan shrugged. "Me and a few of the fishermen use it from time to time when the need arises. We call it our safe house." He winked from behind the sunglasses in a "just between us guys" sort of way.

Sean didn't ask why they called it that. For the time being, he just assumed it was a place they used to get away from their families for a few hours after a hard week of work. Most people went to a bar. These guys had their safe house.

The pilot cut off the engine after he'd lined up the aircraft with the dock and let it coast slowly toward the shoreline. He hopped out and stepped on one of the runners, grabbed a rope with a loop on the end of it, and tossed it at one of the pilings. Dothan performed the move easily, like someone who had done it a thousand times before. The rope tightened, and the plane stopped drifting. Dothan moved to the back of the pontoon and grabbed another rope, repeating the process. He used the second rope to pull the plane closer to the dock. Once it was close enough, he hopped down to the platform and resecured the two ropes to the moorings to keep the aircraft a little tighter to the dock.

Sean got up and crawled into the back. He grabbed his rucksack and backpack then stepped down onto the pontoon and across the one-foot gap onto the wet dock. A coastal breeze blew steadily across the water, blowing his hair around wildly. The cold wind cut through his light jacket. Dothan zipped up a slightly heavier coat and jumped back onto the plane's float, reached in to grab a small satchel of his own, and then returned to the platform.

"How long you think you'll be?" he asked when he reached Sean's side.

"A few hours, hopefully no longer." Sean truly had no idea how long his search would take, nor if it would be fruitful. Fortunately, he had the entire day to work his magic. He had a bad feeling he was going to need it. Concern returned to his heart and fell into his stomach as he checked the timer on his phone. He only had seven hours left to find what the terrorists wanted or Dr. Ott was dead.

He gave another quick check to see if Emily had updated the status of the operation, but there was nothing from her on his phone. Sean had hoped the Black Ring would contact her so she could negotiate an extension. No luck on that front so far. Most of the time, terrorist groups wouldn't negotiate anything. They simply wanted to prove a point and put fear into the hearts of ordinary people. Not the Black Ring. They were after something, and Sean needed to find it before it was too late. At some point, he was going to have to figure out how to take them down. That little detail would have to wait.

Sean walked to shore with Dothan. There was a padlock on the shack's door, which the pilot immediately set to unlocking so he could get inside out of the cold.

While he watched Dothan working on the lock, Sean asked him if he would be okay with keeping his rucksack and backpack. "I don't want to get bogged down with them. There's just a few clothes and my laptop for the most part," he explained.

"Sure. I'm not going anywhere until you're ready to leave." He unfastened the lock and hung it loosely on the latch before pushing the door open. He put a hand out and grabbed Sean's things then disappeared inside. A second later, he reappeared. "Stay warm out there. Give me a holler if you need anything. Surprisingly, I get cell service out here."

"Will do."

The initial part of the walk into town was blustery and frigid. When he reached a sidewalk that wrapped around the city's natural bay, the wind was cut down significantly from the barrier the surrounding hillsides and ridges provided.

San Sebastián was one of the most unique and picturesque places Sean had ever visited, which was saying something since he'd travelled all over the world. The city's buildings, mostly condos and apartments near the coast, rose up from just beyond the horseshoe-shaped beach, clumped together thickly at first, then scattering as the sprawl stretched into the hills and mountains beyond. Evergreen trees grew in patches going up the slopes amid sparse clusters of barren hardwood trees that looked like skeletons of their summer selves.

A blanket of heavy clouds began to roll in from the west, covering the sky in a gloomy shade of gray. When Sean had checked the forecast the night before, it had predicted partly cloudy skies, but no precipitation was expected. Now he wasn't so certain. He picked up the pace, striding fast down the sidewalk. He looked up at some of the homes built atop the ridge looming over him. Their views must have been spectacular on a clear, warm day. Skinny trees and tall grasses blew in the wind along the walkway when an occasional gust snuck by the bay's hillside barricade.

It took nearly fifteen minutes for Sean to reach the comfort of the city, but when he did, he found it was almost a ghost town. Hundreds of cars were parked along the streets and in various parking lots, but very few pedestrians were to be seen. An occasional person appeared, walking quickly down the street and just as rapidly turning into a building to escape the cold.

Another burst of wind, howling through the street corridor and sinking deep into his bones, reminded him just how badly he needed to find a coat. He reached one of the condominiums that he'd seen from the other side of the bay and decided to step inside to ask for help.

Once in the lobby, he found a doorman standing in full uniform, with a hat that looked like it would be more at home on an army general. The man's light-brown skin, dark hair, and matching mustache reminded Sean of one of his friends from college. While his friend had been athletic and extremely fit, this version looked twenty years older, and much less in shape. He stood near a central column in the room. The floors were covered in a gorgeous sandstone tile. A few brushed bronze sconces illuminated the sides of the room while a dome-shaped chandelier hung from the ceiling by a framework of wrought iron.

"Buenos dias," Sean greeted the doorman in Spanish.

The man smiled and returned the greeting then asked, "How may I help you?"

Sean was grateful for his skills in languages. They'd proven their worth a thousand times over. "I'm looking for a place to buy a new coat. I forgot to pack one when I embarked on my vacation, and it is very cold outside."

The man's smile continued to beam, though he flashed a momentary look of concern. "Yes, sir. It is terribly cold outside. You definitely need a coat thicker than this," he pointed at Sean's windbreaker. "There is a shop two blocks from here that should have everything you need. They sell ski equipment and apparel during the winter."

"Excellent," Sean said. "Thank you so much."

"No problem, sir."

Sean gave a polite nod and exited the building.

It only took him ten minutes to reach the building, find a suitable coat, and make the purchase. The young woman at the counter eyed him suspiciously, perhaps wondering what he'd been expecting as far as the weather was concerned.

"Lost my other coat," he explained in Spanish, to which she simply smiled and bid him good day.

Before he reached the exit, Sean took out his phone and pulled up the address for Alfred Wolfz's home. He tapped the link on the screen and then hit the button for directions. A route appeared with a blue line that started with him taking the street to the right, winding through a few more side streets, and eventually ending about a mile away, closer to the foot of the mountains.

He zipped up the warm, fluffy coat and stepped back into the cold. He'd also purchased a small cap to keep his head and ears warm, and tugged it down tight over his hair. With his new gear, the wind didn't seem nearly as biting, though it still stung his face as he walked up the sidewalk before making a left across the street. He wound his way through a series of back alleys and side streets until the taller buildings were left behind and he found himself in an area filled with two- and three-story homes. Most of them had faded white walls with terracotta rooftops. They were packed tightly together, resembling larger cities he'd visited across the globe, though the number of homes was much smaller, making it feel more like a little brother to a town like Barcelona.

A quick look at his phone told him that the home he was looking for was at the end of this particular street. He put the device back in his pocket and continued walking, counting down the address numbers that hung next to the doorsills. A minute later, Sean found the address he was looking for and crossed the vacant, cobbled street. He looked up at the residence, admiring the design of it. The roof hung slightly over the third story, sheltering two windows framed in red brick. The brick stood out darkly against the cream exterior walls.

Sean stopped at the brown, wooden door and took a quick glance in both directions. He took a step closer and knocked, but when he did so, the door creaked open a few inches. His eyebrows knit together in immediate concern. He stole another look down both sides of the street, but it was still empty. His fingers quietly unzipped his coat and disappeared inside, a second later revealing his pistol. It wasn't the first time he'd found a door ajar. Usually, it was a sign there was trouble.

He crept across the threshold and eased the door shut behind, careful not to let the bolt click as it slid into the housing. He took in his surroundings: a square-shaped foyer with floors covered in a reddish tile, almost the color of clay. The walls were covered in something that appeared to be a little like stucco. A few pieces of artwork hung from the walls. Next to him was a brass coat hanger and a tall, skinny black wooden table with a bowl on top. The container looked like it came from one of the local artisans. Its clay had been glazed over in a turquoise and olive-green color. A set of keys lay inside it.

To the left was a narrow, sparsely equipped kitchen. Off to the right was a small sitting area, maybe two hundred square feet. A few vinyl sofas, a coffee table that had to be thirty years old, a tacky-looking grandfather clock, and a wood fireplace were the main features in an otherwise blandly decorated room.

Overhead, the floor squeaked ever so slightly. *Someone is home,* Sean thought, but he wasn't sure if that was a good thing or not. On the one hand, he needed to talk to Wolfz. On the other, going into someone's house with a loaded weapon was hardly a way to greet someone. If there was an intruder, however, that would be a problem.

Sean decided to risk the latter and let the old man know he was there.

"Herr Wolfz?" he shouted up the stairs, assuming that's where the man was since no one appeared to be on the ground level. "Are you home?"

Silence was the only answer he received. He waited a few more seconds, listening to the grandfather clock tick tock against the wall in the living room.

Sean breathed as low as possible for a moment, not wanting to miss any sounds. Then he spoke up again, this time in Spanish. "Mr. Wolfz? My name is Sean Wyatt. I just wanted to talk with you for a minute if that's okay."

He waited again for a few more seconds. There was no response. Things were starting to get sketchy in Sean's mind. The door had been left open, signaling that someone, if not the owner, was in the building. He readied the weapon and moved over to the staircase that ascended to the second floor.

A quick look up revealed no answers, so he put one wary foot in front of the other as he went up the staircase. At the top, a light wooden banister ran along the floor, halting against the hallway wall. A few feet away, at the end of the corridor on his right, was a small bathroom, the door of which hung halfway open. A small window above the sink let in sunlight, though blunted by the blurry glass to keep wandering eyes from getting a peek.

Another door was open in the middle of the hallway. From his position at the top of the steps, Sean could see it was an office, with a small antique desk propped against the wall. He crept around the corner, keeping his back against the wall as he inched his way to the bathroom to make sure it was clear before proceeding any farther. He peered around the open door and found a white bathtub, but no one was in there.

Next, he stepped out of the bathroom and moved down the hall, padding as softly as possible on the balls of his feet as he moved. He turned rapidly, pointing his weapon into the office, back down the hallway ahead, and then again into the workroom. It too was empty, save for a few green plants and a computer that looked fifteen years old, at best.

He kept going until he reached the last door, which was almost closed. Cautiously, Sean nudged it open and let it swing on its own momentum. It was the master bedroom. The four-post Victorian bed hadn't been made, the pillows and blankets ruffled. Another door on the other side of the bed led into another bathroom. From his vantage point, it looked to be larger than the one at the end of the hall.

For a second, Sean wondered at the size of the place. It was a lot of home for one man. On top of that, Wolfz was getting older, and typically, people in their twilight years opted for one-story housing for the ease of use. It seemed the old German didn't care too much for what people thought was the norm.

As his eyes scanned the room, Sean noticed something sticking out from behind the foot of the bed. He took a step in that direction and saw it was the bottom of a shoe. He moved closer and realized the shoe was attached to a foot, and the foot was attached to the bleeding body of a gray-haired man.

14

San Sebastián, Argentina

Sean's senses spiked again, alert to the immediate danger lurking in the shadows. He kept his weapon steady, level, ready for action at a moment's notice. Sean didn't like to assume things, but he assumed the dead man on the floor had to be Wolfz, which meant someone got here before he did. A blizzard of troubling thoughts pulsed through his mind in an instant. He leaned over and pressed two fingers to the man's carotid artery. No pulse. He rose back up, still on full alert, and glanced back through the open door.

How did they know about Wolfz? How did they know where to look? Why did they kill him? And who *did it?*

An overhead floorboard creaked through the deathly silence. He would have his answers soon enough.

Sean put both hands on his weapon and tiptoed back into the hallway and across to a second flight of stairs. He whipped the gun around and up toward the top, ready to fire on anyone above. The upstairs area was much darker. He went up one step, and then another, putting his feet on the edges of the stairs to make less noise. It was something he'd learned as a child when sneaking around his parents' house on weekend nights after missing curfew. He always got caught because his mother and father would be waiting for him just inside the kitchen at the top of the stairs. His guilt, however, was never belied by a lack of stealth. The parents simply always knew, as parents do.

Halfway up the steps, he checked the area just beyond the banister, but no one was there. He continued the ascent, warily taking a few seconds with each step. The last thing he needed was to rush into an ambush. When he made it to the third floor landing, his eyes took in the bizarre scene.

The room opened up into a giant square, very different from the floor directly below. A few narrow windows let light in from the back of the building while a few larger ones illuminated the far side. Heavy, gray curtains hanging on either side tempered the light from both.

That explains why it's so dark up here, Sean thought.

Foreboding shadows loomed in every corner of the large area. He stood at the top of the stairs for a few seconds to allow his eyes to adjust. When they brought more of the room into view, what Sean saw was like something out of a strange movie.

Nazi flags hung limp from poles against one wall where a glass display case contained several items. Sean couldn't make out what was in the cases from his vantage point, but he assumed some kind of nostalgic war crap.

Several portraits of Nazi leaders hung on the wall between the two windows; the middle one was of Adolf Hitler with his arm around a man Sean didn't recognize. It was like walking into a miniature Nazi museum.

He stepped farther into the room, still unable to see into the farthest corner, bathed in shadow. Light seemed almost afraid to reach into every piece of the strange area.

Sean found a light switch at the nearest corner and, while keeping one hand free with the gun, reached over and felt his way to turning on the overhead lights embedded in the ceiling.

A yellowish glow instantly brightened the room. Now he could see the medals in the glass case, along with several other items. The corner that had been so dark had retreated into the glow of the incandescent bulbs. A resounding fact knocked on the back of Sean's mind. *No one is here.*

He scanned the room a few more seconds and was about to head back down the stairs when something clinked from a closet door on the far wall. Sean's reaction was immediate, and he put his gun back out in front of his body.

His first thought was to tell whoever was in there to come out with their hands up. More likely, they would come out with guns blazing, which could be problematic since there was no cover to be had where he was standing. He thought fast, and decided to feign a withdrawal back down the stairs in the hope of flushing out the killer and drawing them into the open, hopefully unsuspectingly.

Sean lowered his weapon, well aware of the fact that the person in the closet was likely watching him. He switched off the lights and started back down the stairs, attempting to look like he'd found nothing of interest. Once he was out of the line of sight from the closet door, he paused and listened, waiting in the dimly lit stairwell. A minute passed, feeling more like ten. Finally, he heard a noise from the room above. It didn't sound like a door opening. Rather, it was more like a low shuck. Then he realized what was happening.

His quarry wasn't coming down the stairs. The killer was going out the window.

Sean pumped his legs back up the steps and spun around with his gun drawn, the small box-like silencer on the end pointing at the window on the far side of the room. All he saw was a foot dangling by the window frame before it was yanked out of view.

He sprinted across the room and skidded to a stop at the window, wary that whoever went through it might just be waiting on the rooftop for him. He shifted to the right and peeked out in the direction the person had gone. Across the clay rooftop tiles, Sean saw the man leap across a gap between Wolfz's house and the one next door. The top of the other house was flatter, and the man rolled to his feet, never missing a beat.

Sean looked down to the street below. A familiar lump went from his throat down to his stomach, filling it with tension. "Why? Why can't I just chase someone through the street? Why's it gotta be three stories up?"

Reluctantly, he put one foot out on a narrow ledge beneath the window and tried to shift his weight enough to keep his balance as he brought the other leg out. He looked out across the roof next door. The man was opening a wide gap between them. Sean needed to get moving, or he would lose him.

He closed his eyes, took a deep breath, and forced the rest of his body through the window and out onto the ledge. A moment of imbalance struck him. Terrible thoughts of falling and hitting the pavement below zipped through his mind's eye. Sean clenched his teeth and pushed off with his right foot, making the twelve-foot run to the edge of the roof. When he reached the end, he jumped hard with his left foot and soared over the span, reaching the flat roof next door with four feet to spare. Unlike the man he was chasing, he didn't need to do a rolling landing. The adrenaline and fear had forced Sean to stay upright. His eyes went back to the killer who was already on the next rooftop and gaining ground.

Sean darted ahead, pushing his feet off the ground as fast as his hamstrings and quads would allow. He kept the gun in his hand but hesitated to fire. The last thing he wanted was to start popping bullets into innocent people's homes. No way he was going to shoot unless absolutely necessary.

He reached the end of the flat roof and leaped across a slightly narrower gap to the next roof. Despite his efforts, the man he was chasing continued to increase the gap, which was growing by the second. Sean peered ahead as he pumped his arms harder. He realized that the cluster of buildings came to an end at the next block. That meant the man he was chasing would be trapped. He considered the dilemma, wondering if the killer would be able to find another way down to the street.

It was impossible to know, and Sean had to decide quickly. He could try to find a way down at the next building and head the runner off at the exit, or he could continue the chase.

He chose the latter, pressing himself to the max of his abilities. His thighs ached, and the back of his legs tightened from the effort, but he pressed on. He reached the next span between buildings and jumped hard. This time, however, the space was bigger than the others he'd covered, and he nearly didn't make it to the other ledge. The toe on his right boot clipped the tile on the slightly slanted roof as he landed, sending him tumbling forward and sideways toward the front edge of the building. Sean felt a twinge of panic surge through his muscles and he desperately clambered to keep his balance. His speed had created too much momentum, and even as he stopped rolling, he felt himself sliding toward the gutter. With a last, desperate effort, he spread his body out, covering as much surface area as possible. His inertia slowed, and he was able to use his hands and feet to stop the deadly slide only inches before his shoe slipped over.

He scrambled to his feet, almost in a panic, unwilling to look down. His body trembled, but he regained his composure and forced himself on. Ahead, two roofs over, the killer had reached the end of the line on a rooftop patio. He was struggling with a door leading into the home, which gave Sean the slimmest of chances to catch up. Sean dug deeper for a little more energy and scurried across the slanted roof. He jumped across the next gap and landed easily on a similar patch of tile work. The killer ran over the edge of the patio and glanced over the edge of the retaining wall, sizing up the possibility of a jump. It would be suicide. He knew it, and Sean knew it.

Sean sprinted hard, intent on making the final jump. He hit the last few inches of surface with his foot and pushed hard, sending his body flying through the air. The killer looked back as he saw the movement and whipped up the gun in his hands. He fired six muffled shots, but Sean was a difficult target to hit. Gravity pulled Sean back to Earth, and he rolled to a stop behind a clay chiminea. The makeshift fire pit was just big enough to provide cover. He peeked his gun around the side of it and squeezed the trigger three times, but his volley missed the target. The killer dove out of the way and flipped over a square, wooden patio table, using it as a shield.

Sean fired two more shots into the wood, but they did little to deter the other man. He'd got a good look at Wolfz's killer in the midst of the chase. He had thick, almost curly black hair. The pea coat he wore looked like something navy men would wear, just as commonly worn at many wharfs around the United States. The face was unforgettable, featuring a sharp nose and jaw with a pointy chin and deeply set brown eyes. Sean took caution as he kept his weapon trained on the barricade. He needed the man alive, if possible. This meant he should aim for legs, shoulders, feet, and arms.

The man stuck his weapon around the table's corner and fired two shots, one shattered the top of the chiminea, and the other sank deep into the stucco retaining wall behind Sean's head. He returned fire, ticking off a few more shots. One went recklessly into the wooden door just behind his target's position. He hoped no one was home, or at least not standing on the other side of the doorway. The enemy returned fire again, squeezing off several rounds until Sean heard the chamber click. This was his chance.

Sean jumped out of his hiding spot and dashed across the twenty feet separating the two men. He covered the distance in less than two seconds and dove around to the rear of the patio table to get to the killer from behind.

In the fraction of a second the two men's eyes locked, Sean instantly noted the extraordinary lack of fear in the killer's expression. In spite of that, the man's survival instincts kicked in, and he jumped out of his crouch and darted back in the direction they'd come.

"Stop! I *will* shoot you!" Sean yelled, but it did nothing to halt the killer's progress.

Sean lowered his sights and aimed at the man's left hamstring. He only had a few shots left in his clip, and that was the last of the ammo he'd been able to procure. He squinted one eye and locked in on the back of the killer's leg. In two seconds, he would be on the other rooftop and out of range. No way did Sean want to go through that chase again. Too many variables.

He fired the first shot and missed, the bullet striking the sidewall in a puff of white drywall and stucco dust. Sean let out a long breath and fired again. The metal round zipped through the man's hamstring and out the other side, sending a splattering of blood onto the patio floor. The killer yelped, and his leg lost its power, but his momentum carried him on. He reached the wall and jumped with his one good leg, but he'd lost too much speed, and the jump back to the other rooftop was at a slight elevation.

Sean watched as the man desperately reached out both hands to grasp the edge of the roof on the other side. His palms struck a metal beam just under the terracotta, and he wrapped his fingers over the thin edge as his lower body swung forward and smacked into the wall. Sean stopped at the low retaining wall and stared across at the man now desperately clinging to life. He kept his gun aimed at the killer even though he knew there were no more rounds left in the magazine. He let his eyes drift down for a moment, but fought off the natural dizzying reaction his body normally produced, subconsciously convincing himself he was safe behind the little barrier.

"Who do you work for?" Sean barked at the man whose fingers continued to slip and regrip the steel girder. There was no response.

The man tried to pull himself up, using his feet against the wall as a means to help his weakening arms, but when he reached up to grab ahold of a clay tile above his head, it slipped off, and he had to retreat to the momentary safety of the steel beam.

"I can get the fire department here to help you," Sean offered. He fully knew that there was no way he was going to make that call. Much less that the firemen would arrive in time. He figured the guy had less than two minutes before his tendons and muscles gave out. Maybe less. "Just tell me who you work for, and I'll call them. I won't even call the police."

Sean repeated the line in Spanish and Arabic; the latter was just in case, though the man was clearly not of Arab descent. He was white. And from the looks of him, from somewhere in the West.

European? Maybe. But there was a more insidious suspicion in Sean's head. He believed the man was American.

The killer grunted as he tried to hold on. Blood oozed down his pant leg from the bullet wound and dripped off his foot and down onto the street below.

Mustering his courage, Sean propped his foot up on the flat part of the wall and leaned over carefully, placing his elbow on his knee. He looked down at the pavement. The smooth cobblestones may as well have been a pit of scorpions to him, but he fought off that feeling and bluffed instead.

"A drop like that probably won't kill you." He hurried his words, knowing time was running out. "Most likely, you'll break your legs or back or pelvis, or all of the above. And when you do, I'll figure out who you work for and what you want."

The man looked over his shoulder for a second and glanced down at the ground. He grunted again and tried to reach up to the terra-cotta roof once more to pull himself to safety.

This time, he grabbed onto the edge of the tile and pulled hard. Sean took a step back and watched as the killer tried to use the piece of clay as a handhold. The man started pulling himself up, which surprised Sean since he'd likely used most of his strength. For a moment, it appeared that he might be able to get his other hand up to roof level, but when he removed it from the steel beam to reposition it, the higher hand slipped. Arms outstretched, his hands flapped in a panic, fluttering past the girder as he fell backward and down.

The first thing to strike the pavement was the upper part of the man's back. His head followed closely behind, smacking into the cobblestones below. Sean winced as the body made contact but made himself keep watching, just in case the killer had miraculously survived the fall.

After ten seconds, Sean could see the blood pooling in the cracks between the cobblestones, and he knew the man was gone. Wolfz's killer was dead, and Sean had no idea who had sent him.

15

San Sebastián, Argentina

Sean had to get out of there. A dead man lay at the bottom of the building, another in a building at the other end of the street. Not even Emily's string pulling could get him out of this one. If he stuck around, he'd be arrested and put away. Corruption in the Argentine government was the stuff of legend, tracing its ancestry all the way back to before the Peróns were in power. Sean was in no mood to try to test the justice system at this point in history.

He took a step back from the ledge and considered his predicament. There was a clear escape route if he decided to go back the way he came, across the rooftops and down through Wolfz's house. That would mean time, and more than a small amount of trepidation when taking into account how the first traverse had gone.

The door to the inside of the home he stood upon was locked. Picking locks had never been his area of expertise. The thought reminded him of Adriana and her particular set of skills that basically allowed her through any door in the world. The only exceptions being the best bank safes.

His head turned a little to the left, and he noticed the hillside rising up behind the house. A hardwood tree stood on the side, its naked branches stretching out like gnarled arms and fingers toward the large home. Sean unconsciously made his way over to the back of the patio in seconds. He examined the tree and estimated how far the fall was to the ground. It wasn't quite three stories due to the hill's slope, but it was still more than two and could be just as deadly or worse than the one he'd just witnessed.

There were three options, and none of them were good.

He heard a voice yelling something in Spanish. It came from the street in front of the house. He'd not seen many pedestrians since arriving, he assumed due to the cold. One of the stragglers must have come upon the body in the alley. Whoever it was, they kept yelling. Sean listened closer. They were calling for the police and for help, which meant it would only be a few minutes or so before other onlookers, and eventually the authorities, found their way to the area.

For Sean, that meant two of his three options had just been eliminated. If he went back via the rooftop, he'd be easily spotted from the street. And if he *were* able to break in through the nearby rooftop door, it would be impossible to walk out without being noticed. There was only one way out.

He hurried back to the wall, stuffing his weapon back inside the heavy coat before climbing up. He kept his body low to preserve his balance, though looking down at the ground below caused him to waiver momentarily. The jump over to the thickest tree branch was a good six to seven feet. Not a huge distance, but if he missed or wasn't able to grab onto the limb, the result would be catastrophic. There was also the possibility that the branch would snap. Sean guessed the diameter of it was around eight to ten inches. It should hold, but there was always the chance it wouldn't.

There was no time to waiver on the idea. Sean swayed back and forth for a second to give himself a little momentum, then bent his knees and pushed off the ledge with all his strength. He reached the branch faster than expected, and struck it with his abdomen. As soon as he felt the limb hit his body, he wrapped his arms and legs around it like a boa constrictor and held on tight. The limb shuddered and bent down, but it held true. The massive tree trunk only wavered slightly from the additional weight added to one of its extremities. Horrific thoughts filled his imagination again; falling through the air, hitting the ground, and seeing everything go black. He pushed the fear-driven ideas from his mind and pulled himself onto the branch, straddling it with both legs.

Sean placed his hands on the top of the limb and pressed down, lifting his body slightly to allow himself to shimmy forward. He repeated the same movement over and over again, inching his way to where the branch merged with the tree trunk. As he got closer, the limb thickened significantly, giving him a sense of security for a moment. Arriving at the first destination, however, removed any thoughts of safety. His next move would be to climb down to the next branch, which was about six feet down and a few feet over. Sean was six feet tall and would have been able to hang down and plant his feet on the limb's surface with relative ease, had it been directly below him. That extra few feet to the right changed everything.

He hesitated for a couple of seconds, thinking the tree might not have been the best idea after all, but there was no going back now. Sirens started whining in the distance, creeping closer to the scene of the crime. He had to act now.

Sean twisted his body around and grabbed onto the limb with both hands. He lowered his right leg, then his left, until he was hanging at full stretch from the branch. His eyes locked in on the next landing, focusing all his energy. It seemed only inches away, but he knew it was at least twenty, and may as well have been a hundred. The ground loomed below, a deadly reminder of what awaited if he missed his landing.

There was no time to delay, especially with the sirens growing ever closer. Sean gripped the branch with fingers like hooks and let his body swing gently back and forth as he dangled in the air. On the fourth swing, he felt confident that his feet were over the next branch and thought to let go, but didn't. He had to make sure. The bad news was, there was only one way to make sure, and that was to let go. His legs swung out over the limb again, and this time

Sean released his fingers. He dropped diagonally down and instinctively bent his knees and crouched over. The soles of his shoes
touched the limb, and he instantly stuck out his left arm to grab
the tree trunk and halt his momentum. His wrist smacked the
broad bark, and his muscles tensed, but he held firm and kept his
balance.

Sean looked down at the next series of branches. They were
much closer together and almost appeared to be a natural staircase,
for which he was eternally grateful. Still wary of the fall, albeit six
feet shorter now, he took the next step, gradually making his way
down, wrapping around the tree toward the bottom. The last limb
was still a good ten feet off the ground. When he reached it, Sean
wrapped his hands around it as he'd done with the first branch, and
let himself hang low. The drop to the ground was only a few feet, and
he didn't wait for an invitation to let go. When he landed, a wave of
relief rushed over him.

That feeling didn't last long. Amid the sound of the approaching
sirens, he could hear a crowd gathering around the scene of the
crime. Making his way up the steep hill and circling around would be
impossible. The only way out would be around the front. A hopeful
thought entered his head. Maybe he could use the mob to his
advantage.

He casually walked around the end of the house on the opposite
side of where the body lay. A few people were hurrying past the
home's corner toward the calamity to get a front-row view. People, it
seemed, were the same everywhere. They couldn't look away from a
catastrophe. It was the perfect cover for Sean's getaway. He pulled the
beanie down tight over his ears and low to his eyes as he made his
way down the length of the house and to the sidewalk. A young
woman and man were approaching at a jog with concerned looks on
their faces. They whisked by without even noticing Sean as he
appeared from the shadows. He followed them with his eyes and
noted the number of people gathering around the alley. Magically, as
if from nowhere, at least two dozen onlookers had gathered to see
what had happened. It was more people than he'd seen at one time

since arriving in San Sebastián. Now, like moths to the flame, they appeared, fluttering to the body.

Sean drifted toward the throng for a moment, pretending to try to see past the people in front and figure out what they were looking at. Someone might have noticed if he'd walked out from behind the house and gone in the opposite direction of the commotion. Blending into the crowd for a minute or two until the police arrived would actually be the best course of action. Sean had used massive clusters of people to his advantage more times than he could recount. Authorities often had a difficult time finding someone right under their noses because they were acting like everyone else. At the moment, rumors were circulating through dozens of ears about a body in the alley, a jumper, and questions about who the man was.

The first police car arrived on the scene with its siren screaming through the canyon of tall homes. The driver screeched to a halt and jumped out, pointing with one finger and keeping the other hand on his weapon. He was yelling something in Spanish about clearing the scene.

Another car showed up fifteen seconds later, coming from the same direction. Its driver parked next to the other squad car and got out, talking into the radio on his shoulder. The people milling around the edge of the alley began to disperse to the farther reaches of the little area, clumping together with people they knew to discuss what was going on. Others spoke of what they'd seen: a bloody mess, possible suicide, and various other theories.

Sean drifted through the still-growing crowd, facing toward the scene but sliding his feet backward. Someone bumped into him from behind as they tried to get a closer view. He shook his head as he kept pressing back until the mob began to thin. He felt his back touch something solid and turned his head to see what he'd run into. It was one of the homes on the other side of the street, forty feet from the other sidewalk. There were only a few people standing on this side, pointing fingers at the chaos, like everyone else, wondering what was going on in their quiet piece of the world.

Sean turned to the right and started walking away at a stroll. He stuffed his hands in his pockets, never looking back, hoping no one noticed as he disappeared around the next corner.

He picked up the pace once he was out of the mob's view, though kept it to a fast walk. There were still more citizens coming out of their homes and the few shops that occupied the area. It was like someone turned on the lights inside the buildings and now all the cockroaches were running.

Down the street, back toward the bay, the herd thinned significantly, and eventually, when he turned right and headed back the way he'd originally come, the streets and sidewalks were once again vacant.

A gust of wind zipped through the thoroughfare, sending a chill across Sean's skin. It wasn't as bad with the coat on, but somehow the cold still found a way.

He wondered who the man was that had killed Wolfz. Did Wolfz know something? If so, why kill him unless he'd given up the information? Nothing was making sense.

As he strode at a near-Olympic pace, he noticed a coffee shop open on the right and veered off course, pushed through the glass door, and walked into the warmth. Getting off the road for a few minutes was probably a good idea. Having a cup of coffee would give him some witnesses and plenty of alibis, just in case.

Around a dozen people were sitting around at various tables in the cafe. Most of them were either reading or working diligently on laptops. Some were engaged in conversations about movies or shopping but nothing worth noting. Sean stepped up to the counter and was greeted by a young Argentinian woman with a bright smile and beautiful black hair that hung past her shoulders.

"Welcome," she said in Spanish. "What would you like today?"

"An Americano, please," he answered in her native tongue.

She smiled at his request and wrote down the order on the side of a paper cup then passed it to the young man next to her who donned a matching blue apron. She told Sean how much it would cost, and he passed her the money, telling her to keep the change. This broadened her grin, and she happily placed the extra money into a small tip jar next to the register.

While he waited, he pulled out his phone and looked up Irena Stoepel's address then tapped on the link for directions to the location. It was farther away than he'd expected, and from the looks of it, he'd passed the home on the way in. He looked out the window in the direction the phone was suggesting and realized that Stoepel's home was most likely one of the houses at the top of the ridge surrounding the bay. He'd probably seen it on his walk in from the plane.

"Americano," the young male barista said from behind the bar.

Sean turned around and graciously accepted the hot beverage. The warm cup instantly heated his hand. He gave a nod and took a sip. The espresso and steamed milk had a sweet, roasty flavor and he savored the taste for a moment before swallowing. The hot liquid soothed his body, and he tipped the cup to the barista who'd made it. "Excellente," he said.

They appreciated the compliment and accepted it with a thank you.

"I was wondering," he said, deciding to appear even more innocent, "what was going on up the street? There seemed to be quite a commotion."

The two looked at each other, somewhat confused. "I'm not sure," the girl answered. "We haven't heard anything."

"The police went by a few minutes ago," the young man said. "That's all we know."

"I may walk that way and see what all the fuss is about," Sean lied. The ruse would allow him the deniability he needed if he were apprehended.

He moved slowly over to a counter next to the window and leaned against the bar's surface with his elbow, sipping the drink for another few minutes while he watched the street. No signs of trouble. Not yet anyway, but that could change quickly.

He turned to the two baristas and waved, thanking them again for their service, then exited the cafe. Getting to Irena Stoepel was priority one. With each step he placed on the concrete, he hurried a little more. He dropped the quarter-full cup into a trash bin and took off at a jog.

If the terrorists knew where to find Wolfz, odds are they would know where to find Stoepel — and it would be unlikely they'd have only sent one man to do the job.

16

San Sebastián, Argentina

Sean's journey to the top of the ridge had been sped up by his discovery of an old bicycle leaning against the wall. A man was standing next to it, smoking a cigarette. Sean offered him the equivalent of fifty American dollars for the bike, which the man accepted. The manual vehicle had cut his travel time to the top of the ridge in half, though the short climb had been more difficult than anticipated. Once he reached the crest of the hill, he was gasping for air, leg muscles burning underneath him.

He coasted down a slight grade toward the end of the ridge that ended in a point overlooking the ocean. The homes up here were extravagant, mostly made of brick and stone. Ahead on the left, Sean saw his destination, marked by the number matching the address Tommy had given him. It was a two-story mansion constructed of flat, gray stone on the outside. The material protected the interior of the house from the best the sea could throw at it, as well as the other erratic weather that could pop up from time to time on the southern tip of South America. White window frames accented the drab, gray walls. The front door was in a recessed entryway and contrasted the rest of the home's exterior colors with a chestnut-brown surface. Unlike many of the other homes on the street and in the city below, the roof was adorned with darker slate tiles in lieu of the more traditional terracotta. A two-car garage was attached to the main building via a narrow walkway that was shielded by cedar boards.

Sean parked the bicycle on the street and walked down the driveway, past the green yard and a row of landscaping filled with nandina and juniper, between two granite cherubim, and up the two steps to the door. He only had to knock once before it swung open and an older woman appeared in the doorway. She wore a light-pink skirt and matching half jacket with a white blouse. The wind gusted as the two sized each other up, and her gray, shoulder-length hair whipped around in a frenzy.

"Well, don't just stand there," she said in Spanish. "Come in, or go away. My hair will be a mess if I stay right here."

Sean obeyed and stepped inside the house. It had highly polished cherry wood floors. The stonework from the exterior was also strongly represented inside with the walls and pillars covered in it. A staircase went up to the second floor, making a ninety-degree turn before reaching the top. An empty coat hanger sat in the corner behind the door.

"You can put your coat there," the woman said, pointing at the coat rack. Though she was being accommodating, she was hardly being friendly.

Again, Sean did as he was told: removed his coat and hung it on the rack.

"Please, join me in the sitting room."

He followed her into a room between hallways that overlooked the bay through a huge, single-pane window. She motioned for him to have a seat across from her in a small, antique chair with crushed blue velvet upholstery. He obliged and eased down, surprised at how good it felt to sit down for a minute after all the activity of the last hour.

"I speak Spanish," Sean said, "but if you speak English, I would prefer that." She met his request with a dismissive roll of the eyes.

"Very well, American. What is it you want?"

Her accent carried a hint of her German roots, but decades of living in South America had nearly done it in completely.

"Mrs. Stoepel," he began.

"Miss," she corrected. "I never married. Is that why you're here? You want to marry me for my money?"

She picked up a glass of red wine and took a sip, eyeing Sean up and down as she did. After she swallowed the wine, she spoke again. "You are young and fit, but I am sorry, dear boy, I will be no man's...how do you say in America? Ah yes, sugar mama."

Sean's eyebrows peaked in surprise. She actually nailed the slang term perfectly. "No, ma'am. That's not why I'm here. I'm here because I have questions — questions that I think only you can answer."

Now it was her turn to be surprised. "Oh?" She slid into a nearby seat with red velvet upholstery and wooden arms. "What kinds of questions would a woman like me be able to answer?"

So far, the whole encounter with the woman was weird. Sean had to pry first. "I'm sorry, Miss Stoepel, but do you just let anyone off the street come into your home? What if I was a thief or a murderer?"

She let out a laugh that sounded more like a dog's bark than someone emoting humor. "My dear, you are no thief. And certainly no murderer. I sized you up while I watched you ride that pitiful little bicycle up to my driveway."

"Sized me up?"

"Mmm." She took another sip of the wine then realized she'd not offered anything to her guest. "Would you like a glass of Chianti?"

"No thank you," he waved a dismissive hand. "I do appreciate it, though. I don't drink."

"Ah. Never trust a man who doesn't drink. That's what my father used to say." Before he could bring up her father, she continued. "Yes, I sized you up. A man with an expensive coat like that is not usually the thieving kind, especially since it was probably purchased at the ski shop in town."

"Why do you think that?"

"Because that coat can only be bought here. They don't sell them anywhere else."

"That explains why it was so expensive," Sean said.

"Indeed. So, you're no criminal. But that doesn't explain to me who you are. So I suggest you do so before I have you shot and thrown into the sea."

Her semipolite nature shifted almost unnaturally to threatening.

"I'm sorry? Who's going to shoot me?"

She lowered her glass to the tall, narrow platform next to her chair and removed a small silvery handgun from inside her jacket. "That would be me, American. And believe it or not, I could easily drag your body over to the cliff. No one would be the wiser."

Sean stared at the barrel. Though he was certain she wasn't lying, he didn't feel threatened, and his nerves remained calm. "My name is Sean Wyatt. I work for the United States government."

A scowl crossed her face, but she kept listening.

"I worked as an archaeologist for several years, so I have expertise in that field as well as in history. I'm here because I need your help."

Sean didn't want to press the issue about her father too hard, but he was the reason Sean was there in the first place. "Miss Stoepel..."

"You may call me Irena." She lowered the gun to her lap, but held onto it just in case.

"Very well, Irena," he stumbled through calling the older woman by her first name. In the southern United States, where Sean was raised, it was considered impolite to do such a thing. Though it had become more common through the years, he still stuck to his guns when it came to the way he'd been taught to treat people. "I am looking for information on something that went missing long ago. It was something from Germany, and I need to find it."

Her eyes narrowed with suspicion. "If you're here to investigate about my father and war crimes, you'll not find anything of the kind here." Her voice filled with indignation. "Whatever my father did when he was with the Nazis is over and done with, and he is answering for that with the Almighty as we speak. People from the United Nations came through here dozens of times through the years, trying to find out what he did or didn't do. Eventually, he died without being charged, but I always knew that he felt guilty about something. What it was, I will never know in this life."

Sean shook his head. "No, ma'am. I'm not here to do any damage to your family name or try to implicate anyone in anything. But there is something I believe your father knew about, an experiment done on the outskirts of the Polish border."

"Experiment?" Her interest was clearly piqued.

"Yes. It had something to do with physics. We are pretty low on the details, but we believe the Germans were trying to manipulate space-time, the fabric of our universe."

"I know what space-time is, Mr. Wyatt." She stood up and grabbed her class of Chianti. He was afraid he'd pushed too much, and now she was going to ask him to leave.

She walked past the entryway, however, and went into the kitchen. He wasn't sure if he was supposed to follow or not, but then saw the woman grab a dark bottle from a kitchen counter and refill her glass with the deep-red liquid. She returned and resumed sitting where she'd been before.

"I meant no disrespect about the space-time comment," he offered, apologetically.

"Not to worry, dear boy. There are not many people in this world who know a great deal about it, even supposed geniuses. I spent several years studying abroad, many of which were in the field of astronomy. It was one of my passions." She leaned close as if about to share a secret. "The view from my bedroom balcony overlooks the sea. The night sky is breathtaking from up here." She could see he was forcing himself to listen.

"You're not here to talk about the stars with me, though. So what is it you want, Sean Wyatt?"

He could tell Irena Stoepel was a direct woman, which Sean appreciated. He didn't like beating around the bush, and from his read on her, she was the same. "A German submarine disappeared from Hamburg just before the war ended. Its name was not recorded in any of the manifests or records we have access to. The boat's name was *U-1500*."

She laughed again. "Anyone who knows anything about German subs knows that none were made after the electric series. They never made it to 1500, Mr. Wyatt."

"That's true," he nodded. "However, in the last few days, I've stumbled across some interesting evidence that points to the contrary."

"Stumbled? You don't seem the type of man that stumbles his way through anything." She pointed at the bulge in the jacket he still wore. He looked down and saw the outline of his gun. "I hope that you didn't bring that here for me."

Sean kept his eyes evenly focused on the older woman as he spoke. "No, ma'am. But I am concerned there might be others coming, others who aren't as polite as me."

She tilted her head to the side, confused by his statement.

Time for him to tell her everything. The sooner he did, the sooner he could find out what she knew.

"Three days ago, a young Swiss scientist was kidnapped. She was taken out of her laboratory by a terrorist group known as the Black Ring. They've engaged in operations all over the world, usually for profit, which makes them unlike any other terrorist cell out there.

"The professor, a woman by the name of Dr. Franziska Ott, was working on a project in the field of quantum mechanics that she believed would revolutionize the world of science, bring about a unified field theory, and potentially change the course of history."

"Sounds like whatever she was working on was big," Stoepel stated the obvious.

"Yes. It was."

She leaned forward in her chair putting an elbow on her knee. "What does any of this have to do with me, my father, and a German submarine, Mr. Wyatt?"

Sean took a deep breath and explained the story about the experiment in Poland, all the scientists that were executed, the one that had escaped with the help of a renegade Nazi soldier, and how he believed the device known as die Glocke had been transported to Hamburg, placed on a ship, and sailed across the Atlantic to Argentina.

Stoepel listened intently until he finished the tale. When he had, she shifted back against the chair and took another sip of her wine. "Well, that is quite a story."

"That's not all," he added. "An American destroyer claimed they had an encounter with a mysterious U-boat off the northeastern tip of South America. The thing appeared out of nowhere, sent all their electronics haywire, and then disappeared again."

"Seems like a ghost story to me," she said.

"One that an entire crew witnessed."

"That may be, Mr. Wyatt, but my father never mentioned anything about a device like that or coming over here on a submarine. It's true that he escaped the war and came to Argentina, along with several of the German high command. That is no secret to anybody. Books and movies are filled with fanciful tales about such things. We did not try to hide the fact that we were German. My father got rid of all his Nazi possessions, but everyone in this town knew where we came from, and they welcomed us. They treated us well because they were willing to forgive what the members of the Third Reich had done. My father did horrible things, and for that I am ashamed."

He wasn't sure where to go next with the line of questions. It seemed Stoepel was another dead end. The term caused him to think of Dr. Ott. He glanced over at the clock against the wall. He only had four more hours until the deadline.

"Miss Stoepel, these terrorists are going to kill Dr. Ott if I don't find whatever it is they're looking for. She's an innocent person. Are you sure there's nothing you can remember about your childhood or anything your father might have said or left behind that might give a clue as to the whereabouts of this thing?"

Her expression changed to one of sympathy. "Perhaps if I can help you, it will atone for some of my father's sins."

A glimmer of hope shone through the room.

She stood up, sure to remember her glass of Chianti. "Come this way. My study is upstairs. All of my father's belongings are there. If he left anything that would give us a clue as to where this thing you call die Glocke might be, it would be in that room."

17

San Sebastián, Argentina

Sean ascended the stairs, following the woman closely. He gave a precautionary look back, making sure no one else was following. They'd been alone the entire time he'd been there, but it was always possible that someone had snuck in. The area behind them remained empty, though.

"This house was built in the late 1800s by a wealthy Spaniard. His family sold it to my father when they came upon hard times. Father had acquired a great deal of wealth during the war and had wisely traded Nazi currency for gold."

"Smart," Sean said, admiring some of the paintings that lined the stairwell. The man had good taste in art as well as good financial sense, despite being a Nazi.

"Yes. Father knew that Hitler's days were numbered, though he would have willed the Führer to live a thousand years. When the war turned, he saw the writing on the wall. He knew it was only a matter of time before the Führer's empire collapsed. He had no intention of being bankrupt when it did."

She turned left and led him down a long, wood-paneled hallway adorned with several more paintings. These were of people from the past: a gallant nineteenth century German military officer, a red-haired woman in a pink dress, portraits of children from the early 1900s, and a few pictures filled with a family.

"This was my father's family before the war. His mother and father, brother and sister, and they all lived in Bayern, one of the most beautiful areas in the world."

Sean had to agree, and now that she mentioned it, he recognized some of the mountain ranges in the backdrops of the portraits. "Bayern is certainly full of spectacular scenery."

She turned her head toward him as she floated along. "You've been there?"

"Yes, ma'am. I've been all over the world. I have to say that some parts of Germany can stand up to some of the planet's most scenic places."

She smiled at his comment, clearly pleased to hear it. "I agree, though I have only been to my family's homeland a few times. Being the daughter of a former SS officer can make travel somewhat ... tricky."

He had to admit he'd never thought about it like that before.

"Fortunately," she went on, "I was able to take in the German countryside a few times before resigning to my life here."

"There could be worse places to retire," Sean said, walking past a window that gave a spectacular view of the crashing white tops of the ocean waves.

"You are most certainly right about that," she agreed.

"Your English is very good." He changed the subject to something he'd noticed before.

"Thank you. I was taught by an American schoolteacher. He had retired to San Sebastián to open a bookstore. When I was four years old, my father took me to his shop and introduced me. I spent the next several years going to that bookshop every day to learn. It's why I use conjunctions unlike many other people with European roots."

"I noticed." He passed her a sideways grin.

The two walked through a doorway at the end of the corridor and into an octagonal room. The wood paneling continued until it reached a bookshelf that wrapped around a massive desk in the center. An antechamber stretched out to the side, giving another extraordinary view of the coastline and the crescent-shaped bay down below. He returned his gaze to the interior and looked upon the area behind the desk. The bookcases ended with the three panels that cradled the desk chair. On the paneled walls hung three paintings, each placed next to each other. They were of three islands, though not tropical. They appeared more barren than anything else, difficult places to live. The rocky, jagged shores were clearly not for sunbathing, and the gray skies in the background depicted something that looked more like an alien world. He noticed that in the center painting, the sun had managed to crack through the cloud cover and a single beam of light streaked down to a place amid the soaking wet rocks and craggy coastline.

Irena flitted around behind the desk and opened a file drawer on the bottom right, then bent down and removed a black leather notebook. "This was my father's. If he left anything of record related to your quest, it would be in here." She noticed Sean staring at the paintings. "A small outcropping of islands between here and the Falkland's," she said. "Never understood what my father liked so much about those paintings."

"You kept them here in his memory?"

"Yes. I may be a snippy old woman, but I do have moments of sentimental feelings."

"You're not that old," Sean said with utmost sincerity.

"I am sixty-eight, and you let me know how old you feel when you hit that age. I know by years I'm still young, but I certainly don't feel it."

He smiled. It wasn't the first time he'd heard that line before, and he doubted it would be the last. He stepped around behind the desk and stood next to her. His nostrils filled with the flowery scent of her perfume. He picked up the notebook and began reading through it. Everything was in German, but much more legible than what he'd read in Poland.

"Do you need me to translate?" she asked in a kind tone, leaning over his shoulder.

"No, ma'am. I speak and read German," he answered in perfect German with a central mountain region accent.

Her eyebrows flicked up for a second. "Impressive. You apparently speak several languages."

His eyes continued to scan the pages quickly. Several minutes went by and turned into dozens as he pored through the pages. Irena eventually tired of standing and made her way to a leather club chair in the corner underneath volumes of old books. When Sean finished reading, her glass was empty, and his eyes tired.

"Did you find what you were looking for?"

He shook his head. "This is just a bunch of notes about his time in the army. There's no mention of the experiments in Poland, U-boats, the journey here. There's nothing." His voice trailed off, and he tried not to sound too downtrodden, but it was difficult to mask. He'd taken a huge gamble coming to Argentina. If the notebook in his hands was all there was to be found, he'd made his bets and lost. Dr. Ott's life was hanging in the balance, and time was running out.

"Are you sure there's nothing else?" he asked, beginning to hit the point of desperation.

She shifted the empty glass to the other hand and scratched the skin next to her left eye. "Like I said, my father disposed of anything related to his time with the Nazis, either before I was born or when I was so young I don't remember. Either way, I haven't seen anything in this home that might help you. If it's not in that book, I'm afraid there's nothing I can do."

Sean's face curled as he pressed his mind to think. There had to be a connection. A worrisome thought popped into his head. What if Stoepel wasn't the one with the connection? What if it was Wolfz? Right now, the police would be scouring the area after finding the killer dead on the street. They'd likely be going door-to-door, gathering information. Then he had an idea.

"Irena," he forced out the first name awkwardly, "do you know any other Germans living in the area with similar backgrounds to yours?"

One of her eyebrows rose a quarter inch. "By similar backgrounds I'm assuming you mean with parents who were in the Third Reich?"

He nodded.

"There were only a few in this area a decade after the war ended. Some were arrested and charged for war crimes, mostly the higher-ranking officers. After the extradition, the small number that remained was left to live out their lives with the guilt of what they'd done."

Sean listened closely before he asked his next question. "You don't, by any chance, know a man named Alfred Wolfz, do you?"

Irena glanced down at her wine glass. Her finger unconsciously ran around the rim in a circle, making a quiet squeaking sound. "Alfred Wolfz was the son of an SS officer, from what I understand. His father was taken away when he was twenty, the result of an ongoing inquisition. Alfred was left with a small estate and enough money to survive. Last I heard, he lives somewhere in town en route to the mountain resorts. I haven't seen him in years, despite San Sebastián being a relatively small city. Part of that is by design."

Sean's eyes narrowed, and his brow wrinkled together.

She answered his question before he could ask. "Alfred is not a kind person, although I believe much of his attitude and countenance is derived from being relieved of his father in such a traumatic way. His mother killed herself shortly after, throwing herself into the ocean from the cliffs not far from here." The finger outlining the rim of the glass pointed to a vague spot somewhere beyond the mansion's exterior. "After all that, I'm not surprised that Alfred became bitter. In fact," her voice got quieter, more secretive, "I think deep down Alfred always honored his father's Nazi heritage."

Sean immediately thought of the odd museum in the top of Wolfz's home, a creepy tribute to the Third Reich that he kept hidden from the rest of the world. It wouldn't be hidden for long.

"If Wolfz knew anything," Sean said, setting the book down and stepping back around the corner of the desk, "it won't help us now. He was murdered."

Irena's face contorted into a scowl. "What? When?"

"Less than an hour ago. I went to visit him before I came here. He'd been shot. He was already dead when I arrived. There was nothing I could do. The killer was still in the house." Sean relayed the harrowing story of the rooftop chase, the shootout, and the man's demise as he tried to escape but instead fell to his death.

Her eyes stared vacantly through the wall just behind Sean and to his right. "I thought I heard the sirens, but didn't know what all the fuss was about. This city is usually very peaceful." The room grew silent for a moment. The only sounds were the ticking of a clock that hung behind the desk and the wind howling through the shutters outside. Irena was pensive for a minute before she spoke again. When she did, she peered at Sean with a look she'd not shown before: worry. "Do you think the people who killed Wolfz will come after me?"

Sean forced a comforting grin onto his face. "It's possible. But I'm not going to let them hurt you."

She motioned to the outline of his weapon again. "With that?"

The question reminded him of his lack of ammo. "Actually," he said, forlorn, "this thing is useless without any bullets. But we'll figure something out. You may need to lie low for a while. Is there anywhere you can go and hide out?"

"Yes," she nodded. "I have a cousin in Montevideo up in Uruguay. I can stay with them for as long as I need."

"That might be a good idea."

"What about your Swiss scientist? Are the terrorists going to kill her?"

He crossed his arms and stared at the floor, his mind conjuring up visions of somehow rescuing Dr. Ott. The visions, however, were blurry. He had no idea where she was or how to convince the terrorists to give him more time.

He walked over to the end of the antechamber that protruded off the main building and stopped at the window. He gazed out at the setting. Gray clouds filled the sky, rolling in at a jet's pace. The skiers would be happy. From the looks of it, their slopes would soon be getting another several inches of powder.

"I'm sorry I can't be of more help," Irena said, still sitting in her chair back in the study. Her voice reverberated through the area.

Sean's eyes drifted from one window to the other. The designer of the little sitting space had created an area with a 180-degree view of the bay and ocean beyond. He squinted to focus his vision farther into the distance. On the horizon, he saw the rough outline of three shapes. From his current position, they seemed small, but he was certain they were fairly large land masses.

"Are those islands out there, off to the east, the ones from the paintings?" he asked out of vague curiosity.

"Yes. As I said, I have no idea what my father liked about them. Ugly, worthless plots of land. He bought them when I was young."

Something sparked inside Sean's head. His heart pounded faster, and his breath quickened. "Did you say he bought them?"

She gave a nonchalant nod. "Yes, though I have no idea why. The land is worthless. It would be hard to build anything out there, and the weather is so unpredictable out that far. Living there would be nightmarish."

Sean paced around the room for a second, back and forth in front of the desk. "That room over there with the three windows," he pointed at the antechamber. "That wasn't an original part of the building's structure, was it?"

She shook her head, suddenly seeing how frantic he'd become. "No. He built onto it when I was a young girl. That's why the stone is a different color to the rest of the house." The last fact was one he'd not been able to observe since the viewing room was in the back of the house and he'd come in through the front. Still, the interior was slightly different, and the seam in the floor told him that there had once been an external wall there.

He stopped pacing in front of the desk and turned to face the wall behind it. The three paintings loomed silently, offering more now than they did half an hour before.

"That's it," he said after staring for thirty seconds at all three pictures.

He moved around behind the desk and slid the chair into its

place. Standing close to the painting in the middle, he focused all his attention on it. "This beam of light right here." He pointed at the needle of sunlight that cracked through the clouds of the scene and shone onto a point in the rocky coast. "Why is the sun shining in this picture and not the others?"

She rolled her shoulders. "To be honest, I never really thought much about it. What are you getting at?" She got up, leaving her empty glass on the chair's arm and sauntered over to where he was standing. Her eyes probed the painting, searching for answers to questions she didn't know.

"Don't you see?" Sean asked. "There is something about this island, something your father wanted to keep secret but always wanted to keep an eye on. And he left a clue to its importance in this picture. I think that whatever it is the terrorists want might be somewhere here." He tapped the painting on the point where the yellow beam of light touched the rocks.

Irena shook her head. "That can't be right, Sean. There's nothing there. He took me out past those islands many times on our boat when we were young. It's nothing but rocks piled on top of more rocks. This place you're pointing at is a rock wall about fifteen feet high."

He took a deep breath and kept gazing at the image. "No cave? Nothing of note?"

"No," she shook her head again slowly.

The answer was right in front of him, and he knew it. He just couldn't see it. He took another look at the other two paintings, just to make sure he wasn't missing anything, and then came back to the one in the middle. He was about to give up and sit back down when something stuck out to him. It was small, almost unnoticeable. It could have been mistaken for a piece of driftwood, a tree branch sticking out of the water, or maybe a simple scratch in the paint that had occurred from moving the picture around. But to Sean, he knew exactly what it was.

"Is there a magnifying glass in this desk?" he asked.

"I believe so, in the top drawer." She pointed at the writing station.

Sean pulled the chair back and slid the drawer out. There were two pens, a pile of paper clips, some stationery, scissors, a magnifying glass, and a black compact handgun with a spare magazine next to it. It was a .22 caliber, not powerful enough to knock down a threat, but could be lethal if used properly. He pretended not to notice the weapon, and picked up the glass instead.

Holding the circular reading device a couple of inches from the painting, he stared at the object sticking out of the water. It came into clear focus in a matter of seconds.

"See?" he asked. "I think this is our spot. And there's a reason you never noticed anything." He tapped the canvas again. "That's a periscope. The U-boat's hiding place is in an underwater cave."

18

San Sebastián, Argentina

"I don't understand," Irena said. "Why would my father want to hide that? And why there?"

"The people involved with the project who truly appreciated the magnitude of what they were doing understood that what they were working on could be one of the most dangerous devices in the history of mankind. Had the Germans been successful, the entire course of the world would have been altered. That fear is what caused men like your father and others to want to keep it from the Allies at first, and eventually other evil men like Hitler."

She took in the information as fast as it came, processing what Sean was saying. "All the boat trips out to those islands. They never made any sense until now. Father would take us out there on random days. He made it seem like a Sunday outing. Now it all makes sense."

"The room was built so he could keep watch of the island. The boat trips were to make sure that no one had been tampering with the location or nosing around. And these paintings were created in case he died and you or any other relatives were ever clever enough to figure out what they meant."

A disappointed smile creased one side of her lips. "It would appear I am not clever enough, Sean. But it seems you are."

He blushed. "It's kind of my thing. I look for answers where it looks like there aren't any."

"It certainly is your thing, Sean," a new voice interrupted the two. Sean spun around first, followed more slowly by Irena.

Four men in black neoprene turtlenecks and matching cargo pants stood just inside the doorway. Each of them held SIG Sauer pistols, the barrels pointed directly at Sean and Irena. In the middle of their formation was an older man in a thick, black winter coat and gray pants.

Sean recognized him immediately.

It was a face that had occasionally been featured on the news in the United States, and one that was often in the same room as the president.

"Bravo, Sean," he said in a mocking tone as he took a slow step forward. "I knew that Emily would go to you. You were always her golden boy. When I heard you'd been put back on her little list of rogue agents, I figured you would be the one she chose for this. I have to admit, I love it when everything goes according to plan."

"What plan, Admiral?"

Sean's stare could have cut through stone.

"You know these men?" Irena asked, confused and full of fear. She involuntarily sidled next to Sean.

"Only one," he answered. "Admiral McClain, this is my new friend, Irena. Mind telling us what you're doing here? And how about you order your men to stand down with those pistols?"

Sean hoped he was wrong. The admiral's entrance came across as menacing, like a bull entering the arena. Sean had missed vibes before. Somehow, he didn't think he had this time around.

The admiral halted his approach and put one hand in his pants pocket, while moving the other one to enhance his speech. "Sorry, Sean. Can't do that. We do appreciate you finding the U-boat. I really thought we could handle it, which is why I had my men try to kill you before. Turns out, we needed you after all. Made for a good show back in the states with the folks in charge. And you led us right to it."

Sean's eyebrows knit together in anger and confusion. McClain saw his opponent was lost in the plot and filled him in. "Die Glocke will go to the highest bidder, Sean. A piece of technology with that potential will fetch us hundreds of billions. Sure, we'll have to sell it to someone on the black market who's probably going to use it for less than good intentions, but that won't matter when I'm sitting on my own island. I'll be untouchable."

Sean remained stoic. His poker face was on full throttle. "Money, Admiral? It's all about a fistful of money? What? Your government pension isn't enough, Admiral?"

The older man let out a laugh. "You know as well as I do that pension isn't enough. Sure, it can take care of the basic necessities. But I'm tired of living a basic, government-funded life. I want to live a little before I die. And I'm not talking about a fistful of cash here. Maybe you didn't hear me say, billions. With a B."

Sean stared through him with fire filling his pupils. "If you don't tell your men to lower their weapons, that time could come a lot sooner than you expected."

Sean's expression never broke, and his serious tone only caused McClain to flinch for a second before he laughed again.

"Not this time, Sean. You can't win this time. These SEALs are going to kill you now. And we're going to head out to that island to recover the sub and die Glocke."

"So for a little money, you're going to let an innocent woman die and put the world at risk by selling off a dangerous piece of technology?"

McClain feigned thinking about the question for a moment before pursing his lips and nodding sarcastically. "Yeah, basically, that's it."

"And you needed me to find it for you because you couldn't do it on your own. I'm surprised, Admiral. You working with a terrorist organization after so many years of fighting against evil people like that. Must be hard to sleep at night."

McClain was clearly tired of the conversation. "Sean, I appreciate that you're trying to stall here, but there's no one coming to help you. And as far as sleeping at night, it's easier than you think. The Black Ring was never involved in any of this." He spoke as if it should have been obvious. "They don't have the resources to pull off a plan this intricate. Although I suppose if I had been working with them they would have. But no, Sean, the terrorist thing was just a ruse to get you moving. And it worked brilliantly. Now if you'll excuse me. I've got a multibillion dollar piece of Nazi tech to find under that island." He pointed at the painting. "Guess it's a good thing I've got dive gear." He chuckled to himself at the last line and turned his back to Sean and Irena.

She had her hand on Sean's forearm. He could feel her fingers trembling. He kept his eyes forward, peering at the five men on the other side of the room. With his lower peripheral vision, he kept the .22 in the drawer within sight, only a foot away from his right hand.

"Last chance to tell your men to stand down, Admiral. Do it, or every one of you will die."

McClain stopped as he was about to step back through the doorway. He paused for a moment, staring down at the floor. The tension in the room hung there like a thick fog.

He barely turned his head when he uttered the words. "Kill them."

Sean was a half second faster with his next action. Before McClain's second word came out, he grabbed Irena by the wrist and yanked her down behind the desk. In the same motion, his other hand snatched the pistol from the drawer as he dropped down for cover next to her. The room filled with the sound of muffled gunfire as the SEALs unleashed a barrage of hot metal at their position. The rounds peppered the desk, but none got through the thick wood, and it was deep enough that the men in the doorway couldn't get a clear shot from where they stood.

The volley continued until every man's magazine was empty. A few of the rounds had gone astray, striking the wood paneled wall facing Sean. He glanced over at Irena who had stopped trembling and sat on the floor in a curled up position with her wrists wrapped around her knees. She didn't look afraid. In fact, the expression on her face was one of anger. Sean didn't see any blood, so he returned his attention to the intruders. He made a quick check of the chamber to make sure a round was there. As he hoped, it was ready to fire.

He knew their next move would be to send two men around each end of the desk. He heard their clips being released. That was his opening, and he doubted they knew he was armed. He rolled around the corner of the desk and squeezed the trigger, adjusting his aim after the fact. The first bullet went wide of the man to the far right, but the second went straight through the quadriceps of his right leg and into the bone. The victim dropped to one knee, clutching the wound with his free hand but jammed his fresh magazine into the grip of the gun by tapping it on his leg. He ignored the wound, pulled back the slide, and took aim a second later, but the shot never came. Sean fired two more rounds, one into the man's clavicle and the other into his neck.

Even the toughest soldier in the world couldn't withstand that, and the attacker instantly dropped his weapon and grabbed the wounds in a vain attempt to stop the gushing blood.

The man nearest him held his gun out and unleashed a volley of suppression fire that sent Sean back around the corner of the desk. The shooter grabbed his comrade by the collar and pulled him back around the edge of the doorway and out of sight.

Sean knew the element of surprise was gone. If he appeared around any edge of the desk, they would cut him down.

"Cease fire," McClain ordered over the suppressed pops of the SEALs' weapons. In the confusion, the admiral had darted for cover behind the wall. Now it sounded like he was back in the room. The smell of gun smoke filled everyone's nostrils as the bluish haze lingered in the room.

"Very well, Sean. Bullets would have been a better way to go. No easy way out for you." McClain turned his attention to the three men still in the fight. "Light 'em up."

Sean couldn't see what they were doing, but a sinking feeling rose up from his stomach to his throat like an avalanche of anxiety.

He heard a faint sound of metal on metal and knew exactly what they were doing. A few feet shuffled away, and then a metal canister hit the wall next to his feet. *Incendiary grenades.* He jerked toward the wall, pushing with his hands, and swung his foot at the object. He struck it hard and sent the thing rattling around the octagonal room until it had stopped rolling on the side. Sean instinctively wrapped his arms around Irena in the instant the grenade exploded in a searing blaze of orange heat. The sound of another canister hitting the front of the desk was the next thing they heard, followed quickly by another explosion. A few bits of hot shrapnel shot into the wall, narrowly missing Sean and the older woman as they crouched under cover.

The wall full of books to Sean's left raged in flaming fury, the old pages and covers fueling the fire. Orange and yellow tongues lapped angrily at the higher shelves until they reached the cone-shaped roof. The fire spread rapidly, and soon Sean and Irena would be completely engulfed.

He looked over the top of the desk, but a wall of hot flames was between them and the doorway. No way to get out in that direction. His eyes shot over to the huge windows. If he could use the chair to shatter the glass, they could jump down. Then he remembered the windows were on a point, sitting atop cliffs on every side. He cursed himself for getting trapped.

Smoke trickled into his lungs, burning his throat on the way down, and he crouched down to get back to the clearer air. "Is there another way out of here?" he asked, not expecting her to have an answer he wanted to hear.

She nodded in spite of the fear on her face. She pointed to the painting in the middle of the wall. "Tilt it to the right," she said, coughing.

Sean didn't wait for her to clarify. He stood up and tugged on the painting's bottom right corner. Apparently, it wasn't hung like a normal painting. It gave heavy resistance to Sean's first effort, which caused him to pull harder the second try. This time, it gave way, and the picture turned slowly like a heavy wheel. The low grinding of metal on metal blended with the sounds of the inferno consuming the study before a loud click came from the panel on his left. It eased backward on a hinge, revealing a hidden passageway.

He turned back to Irena, who was on her hands and knees, trying to keep out of the smoke. He reached for her hand to help her up and gripped it firmly, using his weight to easily lift her from the floor. He shoved her through the opening, stepped back to the desk, using his forearm to shield the searing heat, grabbed the extra magazine for the .22, and hurried after her. Once inside, he shoved the back of the bookshelf door closed to keep the smoke from entering the passageway.

The narrow corridor was made from stone, matching the rest of the house. A dim lightbulb protruding from the wall illuminated their descent. Irena led the way down into the darkness. The roar of the fire became a muffled rumble.

"When were you going to tell me about this?" Sean asked, as he carefully navigated the damp steps.

"I didn't think it had anything to do with what you were looking for," she said. After she spoke, Irena was racked by another fit of coughing and had to slow down for a moment.

"You all right?" he asked, putting his hand on her back.

"I'm fine."

The two continued wrapping their way down the spiral staircase until Sean realized they had gone much farther than just two stories. "Shouldn't we have come out somewhere on the main level already?" he asked, curious as to where they were headed.

She shook her head, passing another yellowish lightbulb. "This passage doesn't come out anywhere near the house. It was designed to be an escape tunnel."

"Your father was worried he would need to get away quickly?"

"No," she answered. "This corridor was built much earlier than that. It goes back to the nineteenth century, built by one of the original families that owned it. Obviously, the lights are not that old. Father had them put in to replace the torches. He used to bring me down here when I was younger. I imagined I was a princess trying to escape attacking marauders, fleeing my castle to safety. I have no idea why the original builders felt like they needed an escape tunnel."

"I'm glad they did." Sean's matter of fact response was reaffirmed by a nod from Irena. "Where does this come out?"

"It merges with a natural cave not far from here. That cave comes out on the coast, not far from the bay."

Sean tried to recall seeing a cave entrance on his way in, but he'd been focused on other things. The two continued their downward spiral for another five minutes, going deeper into the small mountain. The stones that matched the mansion had ceased once they were beyond the second story level, turning into rock that was hewn from the earth, chiseled away by years of patient work or perhaps some nineteenth-century machinery. The wires running along the wall from light to light were covered in cobwebs, showing how long they'd been sitting, fixed to the wall.

A cold draft of salty air shot up through the passage and grew stronger as they kept moving. Irena looked back. "Air from the ocean. We're almost there."

Sixty seconds later, she stopped at a hole in the middle of the staircase. The steps ended abruptly and opened up. If he'd been hurrying and not paying attention, Sean could have easily fallen through. Down below, they could see light pouring into a cave and onto the sandy floor. The drop down was only eight feet, which wouldn't be a problem for Sean, but he was immediately concerned about Irena.

The older woman systematically undid the straps to her shoes and removed them. Clutching them in one hand, she crouched down low.

"Irena, let me go first, and I'll catch..."

Before Sean could finish his sentence, the woman dropped through the cavity and down to the sand below. She landed on her feet and rolled to the side as if she'd done the maneuver a thousand times. She stood back up and dusted herself off, then looked back up at Sean. "Come on. We don't want to stand here and freeze to death," Irena beckoned.

Sean grinned and shook his head. He crouched down low and let himself drop through the opening. He hit the sand a little harder than expected, but was able to keep his balance and stay on his feet.

Irena motioned for him to follow and led the way to the cave's mouth. The ocean's waves rolled constantly to the shore, churning up white foam in the dark-blue water. Off to the left was the pier where Dothan's seaplane was tethered. Left of that was the red shack standing close to the cliff wall. White plumes of smoke wafted out of the chimney and blew away, disappearing almost instantly in the vigorous ocean breeze.

"My pilot is in there," Sean pointed at the building. "We can call for help inside."

She kept close as Sean navigated the hardpacked sand covering the two hundred yards to the shack. He knocked on the door three times before pushing it open. "Dothan?"

"In here," the familiar voice answered.

Off to the right, the sound of a boat's engine groaned loudly. Sean looked around the edge of the doorway as Irena stepped inside. It was a Mark V, one of the primary transportation vessels used by the Navy SEALs. The boat cut through the waves like a knife, its low profile, stealth, and angular design allowed it to move faster than similarly sized vessels, even in choppy seas.

Sean ducked inside and watched from the shadows as the Mark V zipped through the waves and out to sea, headed toward the three islands a few miles away.

"Close the door," Dothan said in an irritated tone. "You're letting out all the heat."

Sean made sure the Navy vessel didn't circle back around to their location before closing the door tight. The shack was minimally outfitted. A small table and two old wooden chairs were packed into the far corner opposite of a tiny kitchenette. The stove was only half the size of a typical kitchen stove, and the cabinets only had three compartments hidden behind bland, unfitted wooden doors. An ancient sofa with torn upholstery sat in front of a black iron wood stove, the source of the smoke they'd seen earlier. A door at the back of room revealed a toilet and sink. The place smelled of onions and herbs.

"Who's this?" Dothan asked, pointing at Irena, who stood with her arms crossed, rubbing her extremities to get warmed up.

She found her way over to the stove and put her hands out to warm them.

"This is Irena Stoepel. She's who I came here to find."

Dothan sipped on a bowl of broth and noodles with a spoon that was way too big for the task. He swallowed a mouthful and wiped his lips with his sleeve. "You look like hell. What happened to you?"

"I was followed. The other person I came here to see was killed. Irena and I barely escaped from her house before they set it on fire."

The old pilot set the bowl down, a look of concern crossing his face. "How'd you manage that? And who followed you?"

"Americans. Navy SEALs to be more precise. A man named McClain, an admiral in the Navy, is leading them. Apparently, he's switched over to the dark side."

Irena cut in. "We escaped through an underground passage attached to a nearby cave. That's how we ended up here."

Dothan took in the information, disbelief written all over his face. He stood up and walked over to the front corner of the house where he had a basket filled with blankets, an old coat, and a couple of toboggan-style hats. He snatched up one of the blankets and wrapped it around Irena's shoulders. "Here. This will help you warm up faster. Would you like a bowl of soup?"

She smiled at him but politely declined.

He returned his attention to Sean. "You're lucky to be alive. Navy SEALs are no joke. They're the best of the best."

"So I've heard."

"If what you're saying is true, and some of them have gone rogue, it'll be hard for anyone to stop them, whatever it is they're doing."

"Dothan," Sean interrupted the kind moment, "I need you to take me out to some islands a few miles to the east. There are three fairly close together. Do you know which ones I'm talking about?"

"Yeah. There's nothing out there, though. Just a bunch of rocky patches of land. Planning on doing some sightseeing?"

"Not really. It's time to put an end to this. I don't suppose you know where I could get some scuba gear and ammunition."

Dothan's right eyebrow rose as the corner of his mouth stretched to a grin. "Scuba gear? There's a place in town that sells dive equipment. They should have everything you would need. You're crazy to take on a bunch of SEALs, especially in their preferred habitat. I can get you out there, but after that, I don't know if I'll be much help. If they try to take out my plane, I'll have to bug out quick."

"Yeah, I know."

The pilot nodded. He thought about the prospects for a minute, pining over the dangers. "All right. Yeah, why not? And I've got some bullets here in the shed." He walked over to a wooden box in the back near the bathroom and lifted the lid. Inside were several cardboard boxes full of shells. "Forty-caliber hollow points okay?"

"That's my favorite flavor."

19

San Sebastián, Argentina

The alarm on Sean's phone started beeping, barely audible above the moan of the seaplane's single engine. He'd forgotten to turn it off earlier when he found out about Admiral McClain's deception. Now he knew that they were probably never going to let Dr. Ott go. The upside was that they wouldn't kill her either. McClain needed her to create whatever superweapon he wanted to pawn off to the highest black market bidder. Without her, it was unlikely he could even get the thing to work. He'd have to have her alive, which gave Sean a little hope.

On the way into town to buy the things he needed, Sean escorted Irena to one of the local hotels and helped get her set up for the night. No one would know she was there because he used one of his fake passports and government-issued money to get the room. She thanked him and asked him to be careful on his mission. She wasn't the only one who was concerned. Dothan had a bad feeling about going up against a band of SEALs. He'd voiced his concerns with Sean, but there was nothing else that could be done. If they waited for reinforcements, it would be too late.

Dothan was right. Going into a den full of corrupt SEALs and their leader was suicidal, but he had to try. It was why he'd rejoined Axis. Better him than someone else. Sean had the skill set to get things done that other people couldn't. At least that's what he kept telling himself as Dothan guided the plane low over the whitecaps of the ocean.

Sean stepped into the back of the plane to recheck the equipment he'd purchased in town. Regulators, masks, dive suit, fins, and a Sea-Doo RS2 underwater scooter. The latter would help him move faster underwater, and speed was of the essence now. After purchasing the scuba gear and a few other necessities, Sean returned to the shack on the coast and started to make preparations. He spent the next few hours examining maps of the island, recalling the exact place the painting had highlighted, and pinpointing it on a topographical map Dothan had provided.

They'd decided going in after sunset would be best. Once dark settled in, any personnel McClain had left behind on the shore or on the Mark V would have a more difficult time spotting their approach. The seaplane was anything but quiet, so Sean had decided that a quick drop-off would be best.

Dothan would fly out toward the islands and feign engine problems, which would require him to land. He would keep his distance from the Mark V to make sure Sean's movements weren't spotted then take off again.

It wasn't the best plan, but it would have to do.

"Coming up on the islands now," Dothan said into the headset. Sean nodded, acknowledging the information. "Last chance to change your mind about this," the pilot added.

"No choice," Sean replied. "If I don't at least slow them down, they'll get away, and we may never find them again."

"All right then. Hold on. I'll give you enough time to hop out, and then I'll be gone. Keep this flare with you." He handed Sean the red flare gun.

Sean put it into his small gear bag along with the two weapons and ammunition he'd procured. He'd already put on his dry suit

before taking off. Now he harnessed the air tank and the other equipment so that when Dothan stopped the plane, he could be out and
moving within five seconds. He rechecked the weapons one last time
to make sure they were ready to fire at a moment's notice. First, he
tested the slide on the .22 he'd taken from Irena's desk then looked
over his Springfield.

"Here we go," Dothan announced through the headset.

The engine started to sputter as he flooded the mixture with too
much fuel and not enough oxygen. The descent wasn't as bad as Sean
had thought, which made him think this wasn't the first time his pilot
had performed the maneuver.

Dothan tilted the plane to the right, away from the front side of
the island where the Mark V would be anchored. Though the boat
wasn't visible, both men aboard the plane knew it was there, waiting
menacingly.

"If they start firing their guns, take her around to the rear of the
island, and drop me off there. I'll figure out another way." Sean's
words brought a twinge of concern on the pilot's face, but he
pressed on.

The Mark V was outfitted with a pair of 7.62-mm M134s, based on
a Gatling gun and a couple of .50-caliber machine guns. The
combined firepower would rip the plane to shreds in seconds if it got
too close.

As they approached, however, the boat did not open fire, which
meant they hadn't seen or heard the plane, there was no one on
board, or they were waiting on orders from the admiral. The pilot
had rigged a kill switch for the lights on his wings and underbelly so
he could fly almost invisible in the night sky when the situation
called for it. Sean wondered how many times he'd used that in the
past. In any case, Sean wanted to make sure he got into the water as
fast as possible to keep Dothan from danger. He might have been a
smuggler, but Sean's assessment of the pilot was that he was a
good man.

The pontoons under the plane began to scrape the tops of the
ocean waves. The plane vibrated harshly for several seconds before

the floats settled deeper into the water. Sean opened the side door and waited for the plane to slow down enough so that he could exit. He gave the gear bag one last tug to make sure it was secure and then hefted the sea scooter off the floor, bracing himself with his free hand on a rung positioned to the left of the doorway. Icy-cold air blasted through the opening, stinging the exposed portions of his face. He flinched but didn't turn away. When he got into the water, it would be nearly as cold. Might as well get used to it *now*.

Dothan throttled down the plane's engine and brought it to a near stop, letting it idle slowly through the choppy water. Sean gave a last, grateful nod to the pilot and eased quietly into the water, stepping down onto the pontoon and then into the dark sea.

The moment he was off the plane, Dothan throttled back up, and the engine began running normally again. Sean floated in the water for a minute, watching the shadowy outline of the seaplane as it turned away from his position and accelerated toward the south, ever increasing the distance between it and the dangerous special forces ship that lurked off the island coast. Sean turned around and marked his destination in his mind.

The clouds that had been covering the sky for the majority of the day had dissipated, and the pale light of the moon began to peer through the cracks in the soupy gray above. With the extra illumination, Sean could make out the outline of the navy ship, about three hundred yards away. If there was anyone aboard, they would have heard the plane and reported in and likely pursued the pilot until he was out of range. Unless, of course, their little ruse had worked.

He switched on the scooter and began kicking his feet. The Sea-Doo underwater scooter was also equipped with lights, but Sean kept those off for now. He would need them once he reached the shoreline and started exploring the cliffs, but for now, his approach needed to be as stealthy as possible.

The little motor hummed quietly under the surface, zipping Sean through the breaks faster than he'd expected. He'd never used one of the scooters before and questioned whether it would have enough power to effectively transport him quickly over a decent distance. So far, he was pleasantly surprised.

He steered the scooter to the right, aiming it at the coast to keep from being spotted by any crew on the Mark V. As he got closer, he could see the dim red lights inside the ship's cabin, along with a black silhouette. From the looks of things, they'd only left one man aboard. Of course, there could always be more in the other parts of the ship, but something told Sean that Admiral McClain had only left one man aboard as a precaution, electing to take the rest with him to help with whatever they discovered inside the island's bowels.

A hundred yards from shore, Sean slowed the scooter and angled it downward. The machine pulled him under, and he maintained the low speed until he'd reached twenty feet below. He switched on the lights, and the eerie blackness of the sea became brighter. The water in front of him was clear for the most part. He could see the huge mass of land, presenting itself as a massive shadowy object just beyond the line of the light's beam. The scooter hummed quietly in front of him, pulling him quickly toward the island's foot. The lights reached the rocky shoreline and revealed more details of the brown-ish-black jagged surface.

He slowed the scooter's speed when he got to thirty feet from the underwater cliff, and turned left. According to his memory and where the Mark V was parked out in the open water, the location from the painting had to be nearby. He trolled slowly along the shoreline, scanning the rocks for signs of anything unusual.

It didn't take long. After only a few minutes, Sean slowed the scooter to a halt and hung in the water for a moment. He turned the machine, pointing it at a gargantuan cavity in the side of the rock. The blackened cave entrance was easily sixty feet across and fifty feet from bottom to top. The upper lip of the oval-shaped entrance was under the surface of the water by a good ten feet, which meant it was invisible from above the water line.

Sean took a quick look around to make sure none of McClain's men were lurking in the shadowy depths and accelerated into the abyss. He kept his speed low, progressing carefully forward. His eyes observed the sides of the cave's walls, and he deduced that while the opening had originally been a natural occurrence, machinery had come through and hewn out more rock to accommodate something huge, like a submarine. He wondered what kind of machinery they'd used to carve out the ancient rock.

Up ahead, he noticed the pitch black of the cavern was changing to a dim, yellow glow. Sean switched off the scooter's lights as he crept forward. Fifteen seconds later, the cave opened up, and he emerged from the tunnel into an underground harbor. Over to the right, a massive object appeared in the water. Its metal exterior was dark gray. The long, tubular shape extended eighty feet ahead to the far wall where the water reached an abrupt end. He could make out the shape of people moving around above, but it was hard to see through the water. He searched the area to the left, away from the U-boat and where he assumed McClain's men were working.

Steering the scooter in that direction, he made his way to the far side of the cavern and discovered a narrow ledge a few inches under the water's surface. He pulled himself up onto the platform and found that it was the first in a progression of steps. Sean kept his eyes on the other side of the cavern as he carefully lifted the scooter out of the water and placed it against the wall on the step.

When he removed his goggles, the entire scene came into clear view. The U-boat was enormous and appeared to be remarkably intact, even after seventy years. The upper part of the hull was dry and showing signs of rust here and there, but overall the submarine looked like it might well be fit enough to take out into the open sea. On top of its stern, an 88-mm gun sat silently, pointing forward at the rocky wall. Behind that, the tower rose toward the cavern's ceiling. One of McClain's men stood atop it, behind the railing, keeping watch over the work that was being done. He'd not noticed Sean as he slipped onto the far shore where the lights attached to the wall barely reached.

Sean removed his fins and left them on the dry ledge, unhooked his harness and tank, and set the gear bag down. He unzipped the latter as silently as possible and removed his weapons, tucking one into the utility belt that wrapped around his waist. Along with two extra magazines of rounds for each gun, Sean had accepted Dothan's hunting knife as an additional weapon for close-quarter combat. The seven-inch long blade was strapped to his hip in its sheath.

He looked up to the left and saw that the steps led to a path that wrapped around the rear of the cavern, all the way to where a metal catwalk had been erected, jutting out from the wall. He noticed a similar catwalk hovering over a landing next to the submarine, a rickety-looking construction that three of McClain's men occupied. Two stood on the end, probably placed there to watch the cavern entrance, except that their heads were facing toward the front of the sub. The other guy was at the far end, staring down at the work being done. An antique gasoline generator muttered a steady roll on the rock landing under the two men at the end. It had to be what was powering the old lights. Sean was amazed the thing still worked. Next to it was a pile of dry suits, tanks, regulators, and other dive equipment, including several black underwater scooters similar to the one Sean had used to get inside the cave. A spare gasoline canister sat upright next to the generator with a watertight lid screwed into place on its top. They must have done reconnaissance before setting up shop and secured the things they needed to bring inside.

He strained to see if he could hear what was going on just beyond the submarine, but it was hard to tell over the constant lull of the generator. Occasionally, he could hear voices shouting orders, but who was giving them, he wasn't sure. He assumed it was McClain.

Sean assessed his plan of attack. The only way to get over to the other side was to go up and around via the rocky path. There, he could climb up the supports of the catwalk and tuck in behind some old wooden boxes that were stacked against the railing. A guard was pacing back and forth on that particular catwalk, but if he timed it right, Sean would be able to make it up there unseen, at least by that guy anyway. Whether or not one of the others on the other catwalk would see him would be something he'd have to leave up to chance. He'd noted that every guard was equipped with Heckler & Koch submachine guns slung over their shoulders.

With only one clear path to take, Sean crept up the rocky path, keeping low and against the wall as he moved silently in the cavern's shadows. He kept his eyes on the nearest guard, making sure that his movements didn't arouse any suspicion. It took Sean less than a minute to arrive at the thin metal rods holding up the metal grating above. Now that he was closer, he could see there was a gap of about two feet between the end of the catwalk and the boxes he'd noticed from below. He hated to rely on lucky things like that, but sometimes it was better to have a little luck on your side than to just be good.

The guard above hadn't seen Sean's approach, as he was monotonously strolling to the far end of the catwalk and back. Sean ducked behind a protruding rock formation and remained there until he could hear the tapping of the guard's boots on the metal grate above, signaling he had looped back to this side. Sean stared up through the steel patchwork as the guard spun around, loosely carrying his weapon against his hip, and headed back in the direction he'd come.

Sean wasted no time. He popped out of his hiding place and began to climb. He gripped the support rods tight as he climbed, careful to make sure his wet shoes didn't slip on the slick surface. He reached the top railing and crawled through just as the guard pivoted around at the other end and started back again. Sean ducked behind the two-high stack of crates and remained hidden. He pulled the knife from its sheath, careful not to make a sound. A quick plan formulated in Sean's head as he listened for the footsteps. Once again, the man's boots belied his approach.

The tapping grew louder and louder until it stopped. Sean knew the man was spinning around to head back the other way. It was the split-second window he needed. Sean deftly crept out from behind the boxes and wrapped his forearm around the man's face, closing off his mouth tightly. The other hand brought the hunting knife up quickly through the back of the guard's neck at the base of his skull, killing him instantly. The body tensed for a second and then went limp. Sean withdrew the blade and let the man crumple to the catwalk. Sean wasted no time. He grabbed the submachine gun from the dead man's arm and wrapped the sling around his biceps. He wiped the blood off the knife on the back of the man's shirt before placing it back in its sheath.

Keeping low, Sean inched his way across the scaffolding, pressing against the wall to stay as much out of sight as possible. When he reached the other end, he was able to see what he couldn't from the other side of the cavern.

Admiral McClain was standing next to a woman. She had short dark hair that stopped at the tops of her ears. Her skin was pale and her nose pointed, matching her sharp chin. Two more armed guards stood behind her with weapons ready, hanging at belt level.

Sean's instincts caused him to inventory the situation rapidly. Three guards on the catwalk across the way, two down below, along with McClain, and the woman he assumed to be Dr. Ott. Even as a plan of attack began to formulate in his mind, he couldn't help but be distracted by the object Dr. Ott was examining: an eight-foot-tall and six-foot-wide metal object in the shape of an enormous bell with various cords running from connecting points to odd-looking batteries on the floor.

They'd found *die Glocke*.

20

San Sebastián, Argentina

Sean's eyes moved deliberately from the three men on the other catwalk to those on the ground. There was no clear path now. Any move he made would risk putting him out in the open. He was close enough to maybe take out the two guards near Ott. But by the time he did, assuming he didn't miss, the three on the other catwalk would fire on his position, and he would be a sitting duck with no cover. The other possibility was that he could accidentally hit Dr. Ott. Too many cons overruled the pros, and he abandoned the idea of a frontal assault. His attention shifted to the nose of the submarine and trailed over to the tower, just beyond the huge cannon on the deck.

If he could make it across the deck to the tower, he would have a clear line of sight to the other catwalk, and the position would effectively turn the docking area where McClain and the others were into a kill box. There were several other crates lying around that the men below could use for cover, but at least he would have the high ground.

The trick would be getting over there without being noticed. And then there was the problem of the guard atop the tower. As long as he didn't look in his direction, Sean would be fine.

He looped his arm through the Heckler & Koch's sling and let it dangle from his shoulder. As quietly as possible, he pressed low to the metal grating and belly crawled over to the edge, letting his feet go over first and then slowly lowering himself down until he was hanging a few feet above the U-boat's nose. There wasn't a second to reconsider. He was committed now. Sean let go of the catwalk's edge and dropped the remaining distance to the submarine's stern. His shoes made a low thud when they hit the metal, and Sean instantly pressed himself down, inching his way out of the line of sight of the main group of guards. The groan of the generator had muted his landing, and no one appeared to notice as he slid into the shadow of the lights on the far side of the submarine.

A quick glance to his right revealed that the guard atop the tower was still staring down at the bell and whatever it was that McClain was forcing Dr. Ott to do. He'd not been spotted. Not yet anyway. If he delayed, however, that could change.

Sean crawled on his elbows, pulling himself along the surface of the submarine until he reached the gun deck where a small platform's coping gave him enough cover that he could go unseen from the rest of McClain's crew as he made his way to the tower.

He kept going, faster now that he knew he was out of sight. He reached the rear of the tower and waited for thirty seconds, catching his breath and trying to assess the best plan of attack. His respite was short lived. He heard the boots of the man above tapping on the tower roof as he changed position and moved over to the side where Sean was hiding. If the guy looked down, he was done. Sean kept his back pressed against the tower's sidewall and waited. He stared straight up, just in case. The platform above him was only a few feet above his head, well within his jumping capability.

His muscles tensed, ready for action. He had two options now. Take the tower and resume plan A, or plan B: dive into the water and make a run for it. Sean knew the latter wouldn't get him far.

The guard above spat over the side of the railing, sending a tobacco driven brown glob of saliva to the edge of the gun deck off to Sean's right. A second later, the man turned around to return to his previous spot on the other side. Time to move.

Sean turned, bent his knees, and jumped hard. His fingers caught the top edge of the tower, and he pulled up, quickly reaching his right hand higher to grab onto the more grip-friendly railing. Once he had that, he put his other hand up and clasped it. He performed a fast chin-up and swiftly brought his legs and torso through the gap between the upper and lower rails. As he did so, the submachine gun hanging from his shoulder clanked against the bottom rail.

The guard's head twitched at the noise, and he spun around, alert to the danger. Sean had already removed the knife from his belt and took a huge step across the tower deck. The guard whipped his weapon around, ready to fire, but it was too late. Sean swiped the sharp edge of the blade across his throat, opening the skin and slicing the carotid artery. The guard's immediate reaction was to grab at the wound with his free hand. His lifeblood spurted through his fingers and down his arm. His last desperate act was to take out the one who'd killed him. As he dropped to his knees, the guard attempted to aim his weapon and fire, but Sean knocked it aside, spun around, and drove the knife into the man's chest, piercing his heart.

He yanked the blade free and watched the man fall prostrate to the surface. Voices suddenly began shouting from the other catwalk. One of the guards had seen the kill and was drawing attention to the threat. Sean clutched the back of the dead man's dry suit and jerked him up, propping him against the starboard side of the railing to give him a human shield.

Right on cue, the other guards opened fire, riddling their former comrade's body with hot lead. Some of the rounds pinged off the tower deck and railing, sending sparks flying as the bullets ricocheted into the far reaches of the cavern.

Sean took a step back and grabbed the wheel on the hatch. He leaned into it hard and twisted the mechanism, spinning it freely once he'd loosened it. After a few seconds, the wheel stopped, and he tugged the hatch open. The circular hatch provided cover — and not a moment too soon, as the dead man's bloody body fell from the rail to the deck.

The rattling of the enemy guns continued. Sean stayed tucked behind the hatch as the hot rounds plunked harmlessly off the hard steel. He peeked around the edge and loosed a volley at the closest guard. While the HK submachine gun wasn't superaccurate from that range, its volume made up for its lack of precision. Three of the bullets he fired struck the target, one in the gut and two in the chest. He wobbled for a moment before falling over the railing to the dock below.

The other two guards split up in an attempt to flank Sean from either side, hoping to get a clear shooting angle around the hatch. He only had seconds before the guards below took up positions on the other catwalk. Then there would be multiple clear shots. He had to take out the head for the snake's body to die.

Risking a look over the top of the hatch, he removed his Springfield from its holster on his belt and took aim. His sights searched the dock until he found who he was looking for. There was just one problem. His target wasn't playing nice.

Admiral McClain stood in the open next to a stack of wooden crates. He had one arm wrapped around Dr. Ott's neck, while his other hand pressed a Glock to her temple.

"Drop the weapon, Sean, or I will kill her right now."

Sean froze, exposed to the two men on the catwalk and the one below. The second guard on the deck was creeping up the metal stairs to flank the threat from the left side.

"Let her go, McClain." He shouted the order but knew it carried no weight. His opponent had the advantage.

McClain stared through him, unbending. "I'm not going to play the whole count to three thing, Sean. Lower your weapon, or I kill the girl."

"You won't kill her," Sean said, hoping he was right. "You need her alive."

"Sure I do. With her alive, I could probably get this contraption working and sell it for more money. But as is, I still stand to make more than I ever dreamed. Some crackpot out there with billions to throw away will buy it. I'd rather make more money, obviously. You kill me, though, my men will kill her and you."

The man creeping up the stairs had reached his position and took aim at Sean from the flank. Sean knew as soon as he pulled the trigger, that man would fire and take him out. The next bullets would be for Dr. Ott. There was no winning play here. The second Sean lowered his weapon, he would be cut down, but perhaps that would buy Dr. Ott a little more time.

Inch by inch, his hands began to lower his weapon until it was by his waist. His fingers let go of the pistol, and it fell to the deck with clank. "Fine, Admiral. You win."

The older man laughed. "Of course I do. I have the ace in the hole."

Dr. Ott's hand behind her back whipped around and extended toward Sean. She was holding a pistol of her own. McClain released her and took a step to the side. Sean's face contorted in confusion, but he put everything together in seconds.

"We appreciate your help in finding my grandfather's work, Sean," she said, her accent leaning more toward the German than French side of Swiss.

"You were never kidnapped. All of this was just a game to get me to find your grandfather's device. Why? So you can cash in with the admiral, here?"

Emboldened, she took a step forward, still brandishing the weapon menacingly. "My grandfather worked hard on this. Why should I not get paid? He endured torture. Some of his family members were executed. My own father spent years of his life trying to find this. I owe it to myself and my family to reap the rewards of their labor."

Sean snickered, his hands still hanging at his sides. As he laughed, his eyes caught a glimpse of hope. He was standing over the open hatch. It was his only chance for escape. "So because you feel entitled, it's okay for you to kill innocent people? Wolfz? Steiner? How many others?"

"Wolfz was a Nazi like his father, and Steiner was an old man. No one will miss either of them."

"Oh, so you're God now?" Sean's left foot shimmied closer to the hatch's rim a millimeter at a time so that no one would notice.

She laughed at him. "No, Mr. Wyatt. I am not God. But at least now I will have as much money as him. For what it's worth, I appreciate you trying to save me." The dark eyes behind her glasses narrowed, and the fingers on her weapon tensed.

Sean jumped over the lip of the hatch and dropped through the hole just as she fired the pistol. Her weapon's report was joined by others as the rest of the mercenaries opened fire on the now-vacant tower deck.

The fall to the submarine's bridge was a good ten feet, but Sean caught himself on the ladder on the way down, halting his momentum. He climbed the last four feet to the bottom and looked around. Wheels, gauges, pipes, and a slew of other controls Sean didn't recognize encircled the room. The bridge smelled like a museum, and the musty scent of time filled his nostrils. He drew the .22 from his belt and looked up the chute to the top of the hatch. They wouldn't be stupid enough to come for him. Each person that appeared at the top of the hatch would be easy pickings.

"You can't stay in there forever," McClain shouted once firing had ceased. "Eventually, you're going to have to come out."

Sean had considered the possibility that the enemies could have been carrying grenades or some other kinds of explosives. McClain's warning belied the fact that they had no such ordnance, and thus, would have to wait it out as well. Still, if things became a stalemate, it would only be a matter of time. McClain's men could stand watch in shifts until Sean fell asleep or decided to come out. Once that happened, he would be cut down like a rabid animal.

He cursed himself for not seeing the obvious. Or was it that obvious? The circumstances surrounding Dr. Ott's disappearance did seem strange. No one had seen her taken from the lab, something he attributed to her probably working late when no one else would be around. Now it all made sense. There were no witnesses because the abduction had never happened. Dr. Ott had organized the entire thing. She'd found a powerful man with the U.S. government who was bitter enough at his career and compensation that he'd happily join forces in order to make the fortune he felt he so desperately deserved.

It was too late to change any of that. Sean made a habit of not letting himself regret too much for too long. What was in the past was in the past. All he could do now was control the moment.

His eyes flashed around the control room. He didn't know much about submarines, much less World War II era U-boat technology. Down one end, toward the front of the sub, was the torpedo room. Two massive cylinders equipped with propellers on the end hung ready for loading. His gaze shifted to the rear of the ship where the engine room was located.

A wild idea began to piece itself together in his head. Sean told himself there was no way it could work, but that didn't matter. He had no other play. And at the very least, he would make sure McClain and the rest of his band didn't escape.

21

San Sebastián, Argentina

Sean hurried down the narrow corridor, past a line of hanging bunks and into the engine room. He spied several knobs, levers, gauges, and wheels, uncertain which one he was looking for. What little knowledge he had about this particular U-boat was that it ran on diesel fuel, which meant it worked on compression combustion. Essentially, even with seventy-year-old fuel, he might be able to get a little power out of it if there was still any left in the tanks.

A cap in the middle of one of the motor chambers came off with a little effort, and Sean stuck his nose over the hole to smell the inside. A stringent whiff of diesel fumes escaped. He screwed the cap back on and turned his head to the control area. He read some of the tags and plates that were attached to various mechanisms and found the one that signaled it was the ignition. He turned the switch, but nothing happened. The batteries were dead. Of course they would be. They'd not been used in seven decades.

Machines like this always had a backup, though. Again, his eyes scoured the area until he found German words for *manual ignition* on a black placard next to a wheel with a handle attached.

He stepped over to the mechanism and started turning it. For the first few turns, nothing happened. Pistons and cams turned inside the big engines, but there was no ignition. Around the fifteen-second mark, however, the motors caught, struggled, and began to rumble, albeit in an inconsistent manner.

Sean took a step back and surveyed the instruments again, finding the one that adjusted the throttle. He waited a few seconds to make sure the engine would keep running. Knowing he hadn't much time, he took the chance and eased the lever back toward the reverse position, just above idle.

The submarine lurched a few inches, straining against the moorings outside. He turned around and sprinted back down to the other end of the ship, past the bunks and control room, and into the torpedo room. He spun the wheel on the port-side torpedo tube and opened the hatch. Luckily, the Nazis had left one in the chamber, ready to fire. He hoped the explosives inside it were still live.

Sean hurriedly closed the hatch and ran back down the gangway to the control room. He stared up through the chute at the ceiling to gauge whether or not the sub was moving. The roof of the cavern remained still, though there was a great deal of yelling going on outside from the dock.

He darted back to the aft of the ship and ticked the lever a little farther to give the propellers more power. Suddenly, the boat jerked backward again as the mooring ropes snapped under the strain. He pushed the lever back to its previous setting and ran back down the length of the sub. At the bridge once again, Sean looked up, this time seeing that the cavern's ceiling was creeping by.

Reminding himself that there was no way this plan could work, Sean hurried into the torpedo room and found the fire button. It was the biggest button he'd ever seen, and marked clearly in red. He yanked down on the lever that flooded the tube then braced himself and waited. *Give it a second,* he thought. *Wait for it. Wait for it.*

After ten seconds that seemed more like a thousand, he mashed the button and sprinted as hard as he could back to the bridge. He heard the torpedo launch with a swoosh as he ran to the ladder. He grabbed a hold of it and crouched low, uncertain of what would happen next.

An extraordinary explosion outside interrupted the momentary pause. The submarine shuddered violently and tipped sideways from the concussion. The ship stayed upright, though, continuing backward. Sean knew that he couldn't guide it through the tunnel alone, and if he allowed it to keep going, it could potentially block his only way out. He rushed back into the engine room and set the lever back to a forward position. Gears clunked deep inside the motors, and the submarine's progress slowed and reversed to the other direction.

Sean's breathing was coming in heavy gasps now from all the running, but he hurried back to the ladder and climbed up. As he reached the top of the hatch, he could see pieces of the cavern ceiling breaking free and falling into the harbor in massive chunks, causing huge splashes that shot up twenty feet in the air.

He crested the lip of the chute and pushed himself onto the tower deck. Black smoke filled the enormous cavern. The catwalk that had been at the front of the sub was completely obliterated, as was one end of the dock. Die Glocke had been completely blown apart by the blast. Now, the U-boat was gliding toward the remaining part of the dock and the catwalk over it. The two men atop it were scrambling onto their feet. Sean could see McClain and Ott lying facedown on the dock's floor, barely moving.

No time to finish them off. He had to get out before the whole cavern collapsed. Just as the thought raced through is mind, another fragment of the ceiling broke free and fell to the gun deck, smashing the heavy armament's barrel and bending it in half.

Yeah, definitely time to leave.

Sean stepped over the side of the tower railing and pushed off the top rail with his left foot. He flew through the air in a dramatic swan dive and plunged into the water. He pulled himself through with a breaststroke, kicking his feet hard to drive faster toward his scuba gear. He floated to the surface and paddled hard with his arms, using a freestyle technique. It seemed like minutes, but he reached the cavern's far side in less than forty seconds.

Another rumble came from deep within the island's bowels as more pieces of the roof crumbled and fell into the harbor.

He grabbed the scooter and his dive mask. No time to get the tank. He'd have to hold his breath on the other side of the tunnel's entrance.

Just as he slipped the mask over his face, another loud crash reverberated from the dock. The U-boat smashed into what remained, driving its nose through the platform. The catwalk above creaked and collapsed, dropping the two mercenaries atop it to the splintering floor below.

The lights on the far wall flickered, and Sean grabbed the scooter, hefting it back into the water. In an instant, the room went pitch black as the generator powering the lights fell into the water. Sean switched on the scooter's LEDs and slipped into frigid liquid.

He mashed the accelerator and pushed off the rock ledge with his feet, propelling him forward. He zoomed through the water, keeping his eyes on the tunnel entrance. The rock formation shook violently as the submarine on the other side of the room drove hard into the wall. A chunk of the tunnel archway collapsed into the water with a splash, just to the left of where Sean was headed. He put his head down and guided the scooter forward and into the passage. Behind him, the roof continued to collapse, sending wave after wave of water into the corridor. He looked back as the sections of rock began falling more frequently, but he couldn't see what was going on.

Keep your eyes ahead, he told himself.

Sean reached the end of the cave's passage where he would have to go under to get out. He pumped his lungs full with quick, successive breaths, and then took one long one before tilting the scooter downward. He raced along the top edge of the cave entrance and within a few seconds was out in the open sea again. His lungs started to burn as he angled the scooter up toward the surface, pushing the machine to its utmost capacity.

He swallowed, fighting off the ever-growing urge to inhale. Sean had never been great at holding his breath. He could do forty-five seconds, maybe sixty if he pushed it; right now he felt like he was capable of half that.

His eyes winced, and he almost gave in when the front of the scooter broke through the surface and burst into the freezing air. He gasped, taking in huge gulps of air, his lungs finally relieved. He pulled back the dive mask and looked around. The Mark V still sat in the water, bobbing back and forth in the waves. In the chaos, he'd managed to put Irena's .22 back in his belt.

Sean switched off the scooter's lights and turned it toward the navy boat. It was time to go home.

22

Atlanta, Georgia

Sean walked across the black marble floor, through the cavernous lobby of Axis HQ, to the first of three security checkpoints. Two armed guards holding Heckler & Koch submachine guns stood on either side of the metal detector. Sean held up his badge at the check in table and handed over his sidearm before passing through.

The next station required a retina scan, and he leaned forward into the wall panel to allow the machine to confirm his identity.

Since moving Axis headquarters from Washington, D.C. to Atlanta, security measures had been greatly increased. The upgrades were things that Emily had been calling for over the course of the last few years, and finally, funding was made available.

Sean arrived at the last checkpoint and put his finger onto a scanner that reconfirmed his identity. A light within a steel panel flashed green, and the heavy metal door in front of him swung open. On the other side, the corridor narrowed into a long hallway with a twenty-foot ceiling. Elevators on either side provided six options for ascending the building. He chose the first one on the left and pressed the button.

The doors opened instantly and revealed a tall man in a black suit.

"Welcome back, Agent Zero," the man said with a straight face.

"Thank you, James. Good to be back, I think." He nodded at the man.

"Emily's office?"

"Yes, sir."

The man reached out and pressed the button for the twentieth floor, and the doors closed.

When they reached their destination, Sean said goodbye to James and proceeded down the sterile, gray hallway. It was lit by brushed steel sconces imbedded in the walls near the ceiling, giving off a pale-white glow. He passed a server room surrounded by windows of four-inch-thick glass. Rumor had it that the glass was enriched with lead as an extra measure of security. At the end of the hall, he turned right and walked all the way to the end where a nondescript wooden door was half open. Two muted glass windows ran the length of the door on either side of it, blurring the view of whoever and whatever was inside.

When Sean reached the threshold, he knocked twice.

"Come in," Emily's voice carried through the doorway.

Sean pushed the door open and stepped inside the office. He'd been there only once before, and the room's minimalist design caused him to think his Axis director had done all her shopping at a certain Swedish furniture store on the other side of town. Everything in the room screamed utilitarian, which he didn't hate but thought was unimaginative. Sean was surprised to see a second familiar face sitting in one of the chairs across from Emily's desk. It was President Dawkins.

He stood up and extended a hand to Sean, which he took and shook firmly.

"Glad to have you back, Sean...I mean, Zero," he corrected himself.

"Thank you, sir. Good to be back in the saddle."

The president motioned for Sean to take a seat next to him. "Is it?" the man asked.

Sean tilted his head to the side. "Like I told Emily, the world doesn't have enough people to fight for justice. As long as I'm breathing, I'll do what I can to uphold that fight. Besides, it's what I do well."

"It most certainly is." The president stared at him for a few seconds with a look of admiration. "You know the directors of the other agencies are crawling down my back to get you to go work for them."

Sean grinned. "I don't trust them." He cast a wry glance Emily's way and winked at her, to which she blushed and shook her head.

Dawkins chuckled. "Neither do I. Which is why I wouldn't let you transfer even if you wanted to. Plus, I understand you two have a special deal worked out. You're not officially on the payroll, correct?"

"Not officially, sir."

"Well, that's fine with me." He slapped his knee. "Whatever works best for you; I'm just glad we can have you when the need arises."

Sean nodded but said nothing.

Emily entered the conversation. "Zero, can you please fill us in on the details of the mission?"

"Sure."

Sean gave a detailed yet concise summary of what had happened, from Poland to Argentina. He told them about the U-boat and the device he'd destroyed during his escape, as well as Admiral McClain's betrayal and Dr. Ott's deception. Then he relayed how he had managed to escape the cavern's collapse, take out the last SEAL on the Mark V with a .22-caliber handgun, and then drive the boat back to the crescent harbor in the city. He deliberately left out the part regarding Dothan. There was the possibility he would need the man's services again in the future, and the less anyone else knew about him, the better. Not to mention Sean felt like he owed the pilot that courtesy.

"It's a shame about Admiral McClain," the president commented. "He was so close to retirement."

"Greed makes people do irrational things, sir," Sean said.

"Are you sure he and Dr. Ott are both dead?" Emily asked the question she'd had on her mind.

Sean shook his head. "No way to confirm, Em. I'd be surprised if anyone made it out alive. When we went back the next day, the entire cave had collapsed on itself. There was no way in or out."

Dawkins looked perplexed. "The device. It's not a threat to harm the environment or population, is it?"

"I don't believe so, sir. It's buried underneath an island where no one lives. If the bell were giving off some kind of radiation, no one would know. Although I don't think it does that anyway. It's unlikely we will ever see any effects from that device or even hear about it anymore."

"Very well. It's a shame we couldn't recover it and put it in one of our labs. Would have been an interesting study."

"Some things, sir, are best left alone."

The president smiled at Sean's last comment. He was right, of course. Some things were definitely best left alone. Based on his limited knowledge of *die Glocke*, Dawkins knew it could be potentially dangerous. He would rather it be buried than some terrorist organization get it, or worse, someone like the North Koreans.

"You are relieved for now, Zero," Emily said, "unless you have something else to add to your report."

He shook his head once. "No. I think that's all."

The president stood up and extended his hand once more. Sean shook it and gave a polite nod. "Mr. President. A pleasure as always."

"Likewise, Sean...I mean, Zero," he gave a wink.

"I'll be in touch," Emily added as Sean proceeded to the door.

"You know where to find me." That was a lie. She wouldn't know where he was, but she did know how to get in touch with him. Sean left the room and walked down the hall, back to the elevators.

23

Chattanooga, Tennessee

Sean sat on the rooftop patio of his downtown condo. A glass of sweet tea dripped condensation down its sides to the coaster he'd placed underneath it. The fiery sunset to the west set the silhouette of Lookout Mountain ablaze with gorgeous orange, yellow, and pink hues. He reached over and picked up the glass, taking a long sip as he stared out at the scene. A light, warm breeze brushed over his skin as the last rays of sunlight soaked him. The busy streets below were full of people going out to eat at some of the excellent restaurants the south side offered. Others were walking to some of the area's bars for drinks with friends. The sights, sounds, and smells all mingled together to remind him of how his hometown had changed so much over the decades since he was a child.

His phone vibrated on the other armrest, and he looked down through his sunglasses at the name on the screen. It was Tommy.

He pressed his thumb to the home button, and a second later, the device read his fingerprint and granted access to the screen full of apps. His finger mindlessly tapped the green text message app, and he was taken to a text message from his friend.

Sean read the text to himself and frowned. He'd only been home for ten days since the events surrounding the mysterious bell and had just started to recover from global travel. He'd snuck in a round of golf with one of his local friends, caught up on some of the latest movies, and enjoyed a few nights of Netflix binging to see some of his favorite shows.

Adriana had texted him a few times and called once. She was in Italy at the moment, investigating a lead on some stolen art that had been taken by the Nazis and given to Mussolini. He was glad to hear from her. He knew she was an expert at her trade, but it was still a dangerous game she played. Sean couldn't help but wonder how long she would play it. Then there was the other part of him that missed her.

The intense situation in which they met had lent their relationship to equally intense passion. He let his fingers play in the air for a second, remembering how her smooth skin felt.

He glanced down at his phone again. The last week and a half had been throwaway time. As he looked into the weeks ahead, he didn't see it changing much. It would be boring, at least compared to the life he'd been living for so long.

His thumb hovered over the keyboard as he hesitated to answer Tommy's message. Finally, after another twenty seconds of considering it, he responded.

Sure. What part of the Middle East?

He waited for a minute until his phone vibrated again.

Israel.

Sean stared at the one word answer. He'd not been there in a while. Might be interesting. He considered asking his friend what they were looking for but decided against it. He would rather hear it in person than via text, and Tommy's IAA offices were only a few hours' drive south.

His thumbs flew over the miniature keyboard on his phone as he answered the text message.

Count me in.

AUTHOR'S NOTES

The device in question known as die glocke still remains a mystery.

There have been a few television shows, books, and pieces of research investigating exactly what Hitler's plans were for the strange machine. To this day, no one is certain.

There are wild theories, some grounded in fundamental science and math, while others border on the fringe between science and science fiction.

What has always been interesting to me as a student of history is that science often comes as a result of fiction. Without the fictional dreams of Albert Einstein, Isaac Newton, and many others, we might not have many of the modern levels of understanding we currently enjoy. Not to mention the conveniences that came from their dreams and later research.

The Island I mentioned in this story that lies off the southern tip of Argentina is real. There are several islands like that in the frigid waters between Argentina and Antarctica. I took fictional liberties with the cave underneath it as well as the antiquated Nazi submarine base hidden there.

I also took some liberties in regards to Sean essentially jump starting the old sub that was docked in the cavern's base. While I never served in the navy, much less submarine duty, I do have a few friends that did, both in a few cases. While it may be unlikely that a person could get a sub started in the way Sean did, it is plausible. The amount of research, both in terms of reading and discussions with experts, verified that it could be done were the circumstances just so.

For more information on the bizarre device known as die glocke, you can see check out this interesting article.

I hope you enjoyed the story and truly appreciate you choosing to spend your time with my books. I can't thank you enough.

Ernest

OTHER BOOKS BY ERNEST DEMPSEY

For Debbie Higgins, a professor and friend who encouraged me along the way. Still jealous you got to see Hendrix.

ACKNOWLEDGMENTS

Special thanks to my editors, Anne Storer and Jason Whited, for their incredible work on my books. Their efforts make my stories shine brighter than I ever imagined.

I'd also like to thank all of my VIP readers for their support and constant feedback that helps guide me along this writing journey. My VIP group is more than just a group of fans; they are truly my friends, and I hope I always entertain them with my words.

COPYRIGHT